"You did. I'm here. You've got fifteen minutes," she said firmly.

"Speaking of timing, tell me when you last went out on a date."

She frowned at him, deep wariness glimmering in her eyes. "I'm not lonely, Kyle." She began trying to tug her hand away from his.

"I'm not asking for personal reasons," he said quickly. "I just want you to be happy."

"So when was *your* last date, Mr. Surprise? Maybe we're both hermits, only in different ways," Sara suggested, a victorious gleam in her eyes.

"I haven't walled myself away—"

"But I'm right, aren't I? You're baiting me, patronizing me. Are you so afraid you have nothing to offer a woman that you have to prove you do, even if it's only by playing therapist?"

Months of frustration and self-doubt boiled over. Kyle grabbed her by the shoulders and cursed softly. "See for yourself what I can still offer."

She murmured an anguished litany as he lowered his mouth to hers. "Don't. Can't. Shouldn't." But then he was kissing her, moving his lips over hers in seductive challenge, putting every skill he possessed into the kiss as he tried to strip away time and bad memories and scars, both his and hers. . . .

WHAT ARE *LOVESWEPT* ROMANCES?

They are stories of true romance and touching emotion. We believe those two very important ingredients are constants in our highly sensual and very believable stories in the *LOVESWEPT* line. Our goal is to give you, the reader, stories of consistently high quality that may sometimes make you laugh, sometimes make you cry, but are always fresh and creative and contain many delightful surprises within their pages.

Most romance fans read an enormous number of books. Those they truly love, they keep. Others may be traded with friends and soon forgotten. We hope that each *LOVESWEPT* romance will be a treasure—a "keeper." We will always try to publish

LOVE STORIES YOU'LL NEVER FORGET
BY AUTHORS YOU'LL ALWAYS REMEMBER

The Editors

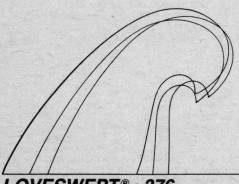

LOVESWEPT® • 376

Deborah Smith
Sara's Surprise

 BANTAM BOOKS
NEW YORK • TORONTO • LONDON • SYDNEY • AUCKLAND

SARA'S SURPRISE

A Bantam Book / January 1990

LOVESWEPT® *and the wave device are registered*
trademarks of Bantam Books, a division of
Bantam Doubleday Dell Publishing Group, Inc.
Registered in U.S. Patent
and Trademark Office and elsewhere.

If you would be interested in receiving protective vinyl
covers for your Loveswept books, please write to this address
for information:

Loveswept
Bantam Books
P.O. Box 985
Hicksville, NY 11802

ISBN 0-553-44019-5

Published simultaneously in the United States and Canada

PRINTED IN THE UNITED STATES OF AMERICA

O   0 9 8 7 6 5 4 3 2 1

For Jack and Ann,
who don't mind having a flaky sister,
and for our mother,
who just traded a lifetime of station wagons
for a cherry-red sports car.

One

Moonspell Keep.

The mere mention of it made the storekeeper fumble with his unlit pipe. His wife nearly dropped a roll of nickels. From their positions behind an old cash register festooned with snapshots of prize trout and trophy deer they gaped at Kyle. They'd been staring for other reasons—the usual ones—ever since he had parked his rental car and ambled into their cozy little backwoods grocery and hunting supplies shop. Now their eyes grew even wider.

"Nobody ever asks us how to find that place," the storekeeper explained. "The owner don't allow any visitors."

Kyle pulled the brim of his golf hat lower over his eyes, pushed his sunglasses higher, and smiled as though castles in the mountains of Kentucky were an ordinary topic. "The road to Moonspell Keep," he repeated. "Can you tell me where it is?"

"Why?"

"I'm a friend of the owner's. Dr. Scarborough."

"Anna's dead. Died of a heart attack about six months ago."

"I know. I'm a friend of her daughter. Sara Scarborough." Again a good-natured smile lifted his mouth. "The *other* eccentric Dr. Scarborough."

"Oh. Didn't know she had any friends."

Kyle hunched broad shoulders inside a gaudy Hawaiian shirt. On a personal level he revered the truth. On a professional level he used it sparingly. What to label his relationship with Sara Scarborough fell somewhere in between. If the memory of shared courage could be called friendship, they had it. If one-sided devotion could be called friendship, *he* had it.

"She's gone funny in her mind," the storekeeper's wife warned. "She's a hermit. Put barbed wire on the walls around her place. Keeps mean geese, trained to attack. Won't talk to hardly anyone. Almost never comes out."

Attack geese? Kyle's amusement held a deep current of sorrow. Except for the creative use of geese, it sounded as though she fit the post-hostage profile perfectly. Barricades and seclusion had become the norm for her.

"I knew her mother," Kyle told the two people who continued to watch him closely. "Funny minds run in the Scarborough family."

They nodded in solemn agreement. "Her mother was a genius too," the storekeeper said, as if that explained everything.

"Go down the road three miles," his wife instructed. "Turn at the entrance to the national forest. She lives inside the government property, you know. Sara's granddaddy built that weird place before the government came along. Forestry service land is all around it."

"It sounds secluded."

"Yep. Take the fourth road on the left and follow it for fifteen, twenty minutes. You'll see an odd gate on your right. Big stone pillars with stone dragons on top of 'em."

"Thanks." Relieved to have the directions, Kyle glanced around the jam-packed little store. "Have you got any Coco-Moos?" The chocolate sodas were one of his weaknesses. In his younger years he'd pictured himself as a sort of southern James Bond, suavely making his request under the most glamorous and dangerous of circumstances. *Coco-Moo, if you please. Shaken, not stirred.* These days he'd take his Coco-Moo any way he could get it.

"In the back cooler," the storekeeper said, curious eyes fixed on Kyle's forearms beneath the sleeves of the Hawaiian shirt while his teeth bit into his lip as if to prevent him from asking morbid questions.

"I used to wrestle alligators," Kyle lied cheerfully. Then he went to the cooler, his mouth a grim line. He ought to be accustomed to the stares, he thought, but he wasn't. He opened the glass door and peered inside. The Coco-Moos, like a fine wine that was being kept for only the most appreciative customers, were hard to locate. He knelt down, drew his sunglasses off, and began to look.

A family came in, and he knew from their conversation and their accents that they weren't mountain locals. They'd come to camp out at the national park and enjoy the fall scenery. Kyle kept one ear tuned to everything they did, even as he searched for his drink. Years of risky work had taught him to stay alert in even the safest situations; a year-and-a-half of retirement hadn't changed his instincts.

"Eureka," he said softly, then angled one long, muscular arm into the cooler and struggled to grasp his treasure—a six-pack of small bottles full of frothy chocolate drink. The roar of the cooling unit distracted him, and he jumped when he felt a tiny hand patting his leg. Kyle fumbled hurriedly to put his sunglasses on but dropped them. They clattered to the floor by his knees.

"Toy," a gurgling little voice exclaimed.

Kyle withdrew his head from the cooler and looked down at a toddler in a blue corduroy jump suit. The child squatted beside him, head down, hands and attention focused on the shiny aviator glasses. A silent litany of curses ran through Kyle's mind as he thought with certainty of what was going to happen when the little boy looked up.

"Hello," Kyle said gently, but knew that his attempt at friendship wouldn't matter.

The toddler raised his head, grinning. "Toy!" The grin faded when he saw Kyle's face. He dropped the sunglasses, his expression crumpled, and he let out a wail of sheer terror. Then he ran for his mother as fast as his short legs could move.

Kyle stood quickly, pretended to be at ease, and smiled his apology at the child's startled parents. As he paid for his drinks he put on a great show of ignoring their awkward attempts to calm their screaming son.

Moonspell Keep. It sounded like a good place to hide from reality. Maybe Sara had the right idea after all.

List. List. Where was it? Without it she was hopeless, Sara thought drolly. Well, being absentminded fit well with the image of a scientist. She had better double-check her chores for the afternoon before she got busy again. She left the microscope and crossed the lab to her desk, where she shuffled through stacks of notes and computer discs until she found a sheet of pink paper with white unicorns galloping across the top.

One. Check phototropism test. Two. Plot new incubation period for the triphilidums. Three. Read article on leaf cell protoplasts. Four. Wash a load of diapers.

"Test, plot, read, wash," she said aloud. "Got it." A sleepy cooing sound came over the lab intercom. Sara listened, smiling, then went back to work at the microscope. A second later the intercom switched to a different channel and began a low-pitched beeping. Sara sighed with annoyance. It was too early for the mail, the wrong day for Tom and Lucy to deliver groceries, and Santa Claus didn't visit in September. Obviously, another curious tourist had just driven through the main gate.

She left the lab and hurried down a magnificent stone hallway with walls adorned in medieval tapestries. Entering the keep's security room, Sara punched buttons on a console. On a wall covered with small television screens, one flashed to life. Sara put her hands in the back pockets of her jeans and gazed at it, seeing only an empty cobblestone driveway by the second gate, the *real* gate, a barricade made of a thick sheet of steel set in the ten-foot stone wall that surrounded the main grounds of the estate.

"Hurry up, tourists," she said impatiently. They must be driving slowly, gawking at the changing leaves of the forest. She pushed a button that turned on the gate intercom and listened for the sound of a car. Finally she heard it. She cleared her throat, preparing her usual polite this-is-private-property speech.

A shiny dark sports car screeched to a stop by the camera and intercom. The car's tinted window whirred down. Sara gasped softly and sank into a chair.

Kyle Surprise curled one brawny forearm out of the car and pressed a button mounted on a short stone post. A bell chimed in the security room, and Sara jumped. A dozen emotions tore at her, sorrow and affection warring with fear.

He propped his elbow on the car window with jaunty aplomb and seemed to gaze directly into the camera, though his eyes were hidden behind silver sunglasses. He wore a light golf cap pulled so low that only a few wisps of his hair showed.

"Oh, Kyle, you can't disguise yourself," Sara said,

filled with bittersweet heartache. The longer scars extended from under the glasses down the angular planes of his cheeks; shorter ones bisected them, zigzagging horizontally toward his jaws. Below the sleeve of a floral print shirt that looked gaudy even on a black-and-white video screen, a half-dozen jagged ridges made paths through the hair on his forearm.

The last time she'd seen Kyle those scars had been much harsher, much fresher. That had been nineteen months before at a special government hospital in Virginia. He had never been long from her thoughts in all the time since.

He tapped his fingers on the sleek dark side of his car, then pressed the visitor's bell again. Her hand trembling, Sara activated the gate intercom. What did you say to a man who had captured your imagination from the first moment? A man whose quiet confidence and good-natured courage had given you hope when there hadn't been any before? Sara swallowed tears. Was there anything to say to a man who had been maimed trying to rescue you?

She took a deep breath, bent close to a microphone on the console, and said as cheerfully as she could, "It's either Kyle Surprise or one of the Beach Boys dressed for a summer concert."

He smiled broadly at her greeting but didn't stick his head out the window to get closer to the intercom and camera, as most visitors did. Of course, a man who had been in Kyle's line of work had the technical expertise to know that she could hear him and see his face perfectly well right where he was.

"Telegram," he offered, making his deep southern voice sound absurdly prim.

She laughed behind the knot in her throat. "No way."

"Candygram."

"Can't accept it. I have candy in the pantry already."

"Florist?"

"I have a laboratory full of flowers."

He thought for a second. "Male stripper-gram?"

"I have . . ." Sara faltered. She didn't have. She needed. Badly. And there had been a time when she would have encouraged Kyle Surprise to make good on his teasing. Her shoulders slumped and she covered her mouth with one hand, fighting a sound of anguish. She could never encourage him now.

"You have?" he prompted her, and a scar moved in his cheek as the muscle flexed under it.

"I don't have." She grasped the cold metal ledge of the console and hung on like a tree struggling to survive a tornado. "Tell me about your stripper act."

He continued to smile his broad, all-American smile that made her think of wheat fields and sunflowers. But something hard settled around his mouth. "Sorry, I'm not in the stripper-gram business anymore."

She hurt for him so much. The scars don't matter, she wanted to tell him. They really don't. "I like your Florida clothes," she commented in a vague attempt at normal conversation. "We never see anything so, uhmmm, cheerful, up here. Especially after the weather turns cool."

"I know why. I'm freezing." He clasped his chest and asked quaintly, "Want to invite me inside the castle to get warm?"

She stalled for time. "What are you doing so far from the beach?"

Even with the sunglasses covering his expressive eyes she could tell that his humor was a facade. It faded now, replaced by a look of quiet determination. "Dinah asked me to come check on you. She expected you to get over this reclusive phase by now. She's worried because you won't visit her or let her visit you."

This was the kind of attention Sara had feared for months. She shut her eyes and willed thoughts of sympathy, friendship, and loneliness away. "I'm making a break with the past," she told Kyle in a low, firm voice. "I think it's the best thing to do."

He shook his head. "I understand what you're going through, but shutting yourself away from your friends isn't the way to handle it. Believe me. Dinah went through the same feelings, but Rucker wouldn't let her give in to them. Now she's doing fine."

Sadly, Sara looked at the television screen. She and Dinah McClure had been prisoners together in South America, true. They had suffered the same torments and fought back with the same bold but useless courage, true. But the aftermath of their ordeal had not been similar.

Sara bowed her head over the console's microphone. Hers was no ordinary post-hostage situation. "I'm sorry you made a long trip for nothing. I'm fine, really. Tell Dinah you spoke to me and everything's all right. Give her and Rucker and the baby my love. And tell your brother hello. Oh, and Drake Lancaster too."

"You mean you're not going to let me see you?" Despite the sunglasses and low-slung cap, his consternation was obvious.

"That's right." Sara stared hard at his image, trying to absorb every detail before she switched off the camera. Afterward she would play the tape over and over, just to look at him.

"Sara, I'm no threat to you," he said patiently. "No one is anymore."

"Everything that reminds me of those ten months in Surador is a threat."

He inhaled sharply. "I know that I'm not easy to look at. Hell, you've heard the old line." His voice became sardonic. " 'What bothers you most: when the women scream or when the children point?' I'm the walking personification of that. But, Sara—"

"No." She put her head in her hands. How could she let him think he was so ugly that she couldn't bear the sight? "It has nothing to do with *your* scars. It has to do with mine. Thank you for making the trip. Now, please, go back to Florida."

"I can't do that, Sara." He sighed. "I rented this car at the Lexington airport. I've already agreed to keep it until the day of my flight home."

"When is that?"

"I don't know." His teasing grin appeared. "That depends on how soon you cooperate."

"Come on! I'm deep into my research. I really don't have time to play hostess!"

"Ten minutes. Give me ten minutes." He smiled tightly. "I get it. You've injected yourself with some kind of plant hormone and turned into a mutant green thing. Can I have the movie rights to your story?"

"Please go away."

He shook his head. "Ten minutes."

She noticed that he was sitting up straighter, his jaw clenched, his hand gripping the frame of the car window. Sara eyed him with alarm. "Don't even *think* of trying to rescue me again. I don't want to be rescued. And I have state-of-the-art security systems."

"Attack geese," he said dryly.

Sara winced. He must have talked to one of the locals, she mused. But she wasn't kidding about the system. It was designed to protect Moonspell Keep from even the most determined invader.

"Why won't you let me inside?" he asked.

"Judging by the trouble my research caused before, I think it's best that it remain completely confidential."

"I don't care about your plant research. I'm not here to peek at your lab or fondle your orchids."

"I told you, I'm putting my past behind me."

"But you haven't built much of a present or a future to take its place. We'll talk, we'll work out your fears—"

"My only fear is that you won't go away."

"That's a valid one, then, because, lady, I'm not."

Sara recalled that his aging-Beach-Boy outfit concealed a lean, powerful body that served him well no matter what he asked of it—which in this case might include climbing stone walls and dodging a flock of mean geese.

He could never get inside her fortified home, but he could probably—no, definitely—get inside the grounds and cause a great deal of trouble. "All right, ten minutes," she told him wearily. "But I'll walk down to the gate and talk to you there."

"Good enough. Sara, the past is over. You can relax."

She bit back an ironic laugh. Looking at his scarred face and thinking of her daughter—whom he might despise if he ever learned of her existence—Sara knew that she could never relax.

Kyle got out of the car and leaned nonchalantly against the front fender, pulling a white Windbreaker over his arms as he did. Crossing his legs at sockless ankles, he stared at his baggy white trousers and white running shoes.

The sports car and the beach clothes would, he hoped, make him look a hell of a lot more jovial and carefree than he was. The last thing he wanted was to remind Sara of the last time she'd seen him.

Should he take off the sunglasses? Remove the hat? He ought to. Unlike the Windbreaker, the glasses and hat made it obvious that he wanted to hide his scars. Nothing carefree about that. Kyle realized that his throat was dry with anticipation and dread. He hesitated for a moment, then tossed the hat onto the car's hood and laid the sunglasses beside it. Running his fingers through his sun-streaked hair, he exhaled wearily and waited.

There was no sound from the other side of the massive gate. Kyle gazed at the gray steel, listening as the minutes passed. It began to dawn on him that she might have lied about the visit. He eyed the stone walls that stretched into the forest on either side, calculating ways to get through the barbed-wire shield that protruded from their outer edge. He looked closer, noting a barbless wire that wound through the others. The shield was electrified.

Dear Lord, who did she expect to fight? Ninjas? Rambo?

"Hello," a soft voice said behind him.

He whipped around, silently cursing himself for being so distracted that he hadn't heard her footsteps. She stood on the other side of the car, leaning toward him a little, her small hands pressed atop the fender as if she liked knowing the car was a barrier between them.

The world shrank, becoming only a backdrop for their silent tableau. Her shadowed green eyes never strayed from his pensive blue ones. Her jeaned legs were braced slightly apart; her chest moved raggedly under a pullover sweater striped in russet and gray. He wanted to hug her, wanted to gather this deceptively delicate-looking woman into his arms and tell her that he'd never forgotten her. Instead, he shoved his hands into his trouser pockets.

"You cut your hair," he said finally.

She blinked, thought for a moment, then nodded. "Right after I came home. As part of my starting-new program."

"Pretty dramatic."

Touching a hand to the short, feathery cap of cinnamon-red hair that had once hung to her waist, she smiled tentatively. "I guess it's a shock to you."

"I'm used to shocks. I like it."

"At least it makes me look older. Now when I see myself in a mirror I don't fight an urge to buy pom-poms and join a cheerleading squad."

He forced a jaunty grin on his face. "How old *are* you these days?"

"On a good day, thirty. On a bad day, about a hundred and twelve. How about you?"

"On a good day, thirty-six. On a bad day, about fourteen. I regress." She laughed, but the sound died quickly. She looked at him in bewilderment. "What's wrong?"

Kyle realized that his face was revealing a lot more than he'd planned. "I've never heard you laugh before. It's a nice sound."

She glanced away, her expression troubled. "Well, we didn't get a chance to spend much time together, before. What, an hour in Surador? A few days at the hospital in Virginia? And the situations didn't lend themselves to humor."

"I'm glad you can laugh now."

"Can *you*?" She watched him closely.

He nodded. "On the good days."

"Do you and your brother stay busy down in Ft. Lauderdale? With the new work?"

"As busy as two old retired men want to be."

"Well, Gramps, how does it feel to run a safe, normal import-export business?"

Kyle considered telling her the truth, but decided that it might make her more wary of him. The business was a front for a private investigations service—very discreet and very far above the average P.I.'s milieu. Their clients included small foreign governments and multinational corporations. But compared to their former occupations, the work was definitely safe and normal.

"There's a lot of money in shipping and receiving European antiques," Kyle told her lightly. "And no one tries to kill you over them."

"You look good, Kyle. I mean that."

His stomach tightened. He didn't dwell on his scars. He knew *exactly* how awful they were, but Sara sounded very sincere. He liked the quality and gentleness of her lie. "I've had a lot of plastic surgery. I'll have more, as time goes by." He changed the subject quickly. "Where's the secret door?" He gestured toward the stone wall. "How did you get out and sneak up on me? If I give you some cereal box tops, can I have your special map and decoder ring?"

Her eyes crinkled with amusement. "The keep was designed to be mysterious. My grandfather was a creative architect. My mother added a few secret touches of her own."

"Which is a polite way of saying 'Mind your own business, nosy.' "

"I'm afraid so." Frowning, she added, "It has to be that way. If I'd been secretive about my work before, there wouldn't have been any trouble." Sorrow flickered in her eyes for an instant as her gaze swept his face; without words she showed her guilt over his own condition.

"You were doing your job," Kyle told her gruffly. "I was doing mine. We couldn't help what happened."

She shook her head. "I could have."

"How?"

"By not trusting Valdivia to begin with." Visibly shaken, she raised a hand to her throat. "That's the first time I've said his name out loud since I came home from South America. I'd prefer never to say it again."

The mention of Diego de Valdivia broke the tenuous spell Kyle had built. She stepped back, obviously on the verge of leaving. "Don't," he told her. Kyle moved toward her and held out his hands in supplication. "How could you have known that he wasn't an ordinary businessman who was just curious about your research with herbicides?"

It was no use. She looked guilty and distraught and more than a little angry. "It's over. He forced me to create something I hated, something so awful that it still makes me sick to think about it, and I don't feel any better knowing that our government has control of it now. I can't do anything about that, but I *can* make sure that my research never gets twisted that way again."

"Valdivia's dead, you know. You're letting his ghost haunt you. You're here all alone—"

"Good-bye, Kyle," she said, her voice strained. "It was good to see you again." She began backing into the forest. "Maybe someday we—take care. Take good care of yourself. You deserve all the happiness in the world. Bye."

He moved forward, grimacing with frustration. "It's not that easy, Sara. I didn't come here simply because Dinah asked me to. I didn't come just to help you. I came to fight some of my own demons too."

She smiled nervously. "Dragons, not demons. That's what I have here. Didn't you see them on the main gate? Go home. Please, go home."

"No." She was still backing; he was still advancing. "Let me inside the keep right now or I'll pester you until you do."

"I won't. Not ever."

"Then you better tighten your security."

She halted, her fists clenched, her eyes wide with amazement. "Stay off the grounds, Kyle. I didn't want to tell you this, but . . . I have dogs. Security dogs. Rottweilers. Trained to attack."

He froze, her words a betrayal, the worst kind. Some of his sympathy for her turned to disgust, and he uttered a few stunned curses that made her wince. "You know what dogs like those can do to a person," she said softly, her voice choked. "You know."

With one last, tearful look at his ravaged face, she turned and walked away.

Two

He wasted no time. He went to the tiny mountain town nearby, bought a tent and other gear, and by late afternoon began setting up camp not two dozen yards from the keep's forbidding gate.

Sara watched every move he made via a network of cameras hidden in the trees outside the wall. She shut the lab down temporarily, then went into the greenhouse in the cavern underneath the castle and set all the feeding, lighting, and watering systems on automatic.

Finally she went into the nursery and bent over the pink and white playpen. "Come here, sweetheart. I'm going to move you to another room."

Sara always conversed with her daughter in an adult voice, as if her words were being understood. As a result of that and all the time they spent together, ten-month-old Noelle was advanced for her age. Seated among her toys, she held up both arms and gave a dimpled grin. *"Roooom."*

Sara laughed softly. "You sound like Inspector Clouseau in a Pink Panther movie."

"Roooom. Roooom."

That was as far as the conversation went, but Noelle

chuckled gleefully as Sara set her on the carpeted floor. She immediately poked her diapered fanny in the air, pushed herself onto all fours, then into a wobbly stance, and clasped the leg of Sara's jeans.

"I should have named you Vine. Clinging Vine," Sara teased. She folded the playpen, scooped one arm around Noelle, and started from the room carrying her on one side, the playpen on the other. "Come on, Daisy." The lanky, golden-coated dog got up from its spot in a streak of sunshine by the nursery's barred window. She followed closely, tongue lolling. Sara knew that the dog would have come without a command. Where Noelle went, Daisy went. Sara's mother had often said that there would never be a more devoted baby-sitter than Daisy.

Sara paused at the door and glanced back at a framed snapshot hanging on the wall over the crib. Her mother smiled at her from under disheveled gray hair, looking both scholarly and motherly. Dr. Anna Scarborough had had a difficult time gaining respectability as a scientist back when the world had said that the mystery of the womb was the only kind of biology a woman ought to study. Nonetheless, she had managed to blaze an impressive trail in the world's scientific community by compiling extraordinary research on plants in remote areas that few other scientists had visited. Then at the relatively late age of forty she had married a fellow biologist, happily given birth to two children, and concentrated her work in the laboratory and greenhouse she built at the castle.

She had seen and done a great deal, and last Christmas eve, as a fitting climax to a serendipitous life, she had calmly served as midwife for her first grandchild. Sara had never worried about giving birth at home because Anna Scarborough and Mother Nature were old friends.

Four months later, while attending a conference of

environmentalists in New York, Anna had slumped over in her chair, her seventy-year-old heart too tired to continue beating.

Sara would always believe that her mother had died happy—in the midst of her work, with her daughter and granddaughter waiting safely back in Kentucky. But Sara also believed that the strain of having a daughter kidnapped, the months of coerced research, and the worry that Valdivia's poisonous life would taint her granddaughter's future had contributed to Anna's early death.

Sara quickly looked away from the photo on the wall. Remorse made her even more determined not to involve anyone else in her or Noelle's lives.

When she reached the security room, Sara set up the playpen and placed Noelle in it. The baby's dark eyes widened with fascination at the bank of flickering television screens on one wall. She squealed, and Daisy perked her floppy ears in curiosity.

"We're going to stay here for a while and watch Mr. Surprise," Sara told them. "And I'm going to try to decide what to do about him."

Daisy yawned and snuffled the playpen's webbed sides so that Noelle could pat a small hand to her nose, Sara gazed at the dog and felt a deep stab of guilt. *Trained attack dogs, indeed.*

Daisy was the only dog in the keep. She had wandered up to the gate last year, a scraggly, starving puppy with loving eyes. One of her parents might have been a golden retriever; the other had undoubtedly been something with no brains and even less coordination. Bugs were the only creatures Daisy ever menaced. She was so clumsy that she stepped on them accidentally.

Sara turned toward the video screens and sat down in a high-backed swivel chair. Her heart thudded as she watched Kyle Surprise finish setting up his camp, arranging lanterns and building a fire with a skill that spoke of much experience. The semiautomatic pistol hanging in a holster on the front of his tent indicated experience of another kind.

A quilted jacket now covered his Hawaiian shirt. He moved with decisiveness. He wasn't more than six feet tall, but he looked taller. He had the lanky agility of a runner, and seemed to get wherever he was headed in no more than one or two easy strides.

His reddish-blond hair was longer than she remembered, and tended to wisp upward around his ears and the back of his neck. She wondered if he had let it grow out to soften the effect of the scars on his face.

Sara pressed trembling fingertips to her lips and studied that face as objectively as she could. He wouldn't believe her if she told him so, but he was still an incredibly sexy man. He had never had the matinee-idol perfection that made women gape at his brother Jeopard, but his features had been—and still were—strong and sensual in a way that made perfection unnecessary.

The scars *were* terrible, especially the jagged one that ran under his eyes and across the bridge of his nose. But his eyes, Lord, his eyes made her forget everything else. The security camera didn't do them justice. Big and dark blue, sheltered by thick blond lashes, they were still the warmest, kindest eyes she'd ever seen. How they'd kept that look despite years of dangerous and often cynical work she had never fully understood.

But then, she really didn't know Kyle—not the details of his background, his likes or dislikes, his dreams. She had been sitting with Dinah McClure the day he'd shot a paper airplane over the garden wall of Valdivia's estate in Surador. He had learned somehow that their guards let them venture into the garden alone for an hour every afternoon.

Hello, Dinah McClure, the note in the airplane had

said. *This is Kyle Surprise. Remember me? Would you and your friend like to split this banana farm?*

Dinah had known Kyle and Jeopard Surprise through their sister, Millie, who had been her husband's secretary. Everyone, including Millie, thought that her brothers performed routine investigations for U.S. Navy Intelligence. Until the note came sailing out of the Suradoran jungle, Dinah had had no idea that Kyle and Jeopard were agents for a special hostage-retrieval group called Audubon.

Yes. Please help us, Dinah had scribbled back, using one of the tooth-marked pens Sara always carried to jot down lists and ideas.

For the whole hour they'd traded airplanes with Kyle, telling him how Valdivia had kidnapped Sara in Florida and how Dinah had innocently gotten kidnapped by association; how Valdivia was making Sara work on a herbicide for military use; how Dinah had recently given birth to the baby she'd been carrying when Valdivia took her hostage.

For the first time in months they'd had hope of escaping. The next day they had exchanged more notes with Kyle, and a plan had been devised, but before he could put it into action he was captured by Valdivia's men.

Sara would never forget her first face-to-face meeting with Kyle Surprise. Like some kind of prize animal on display, he was chained by the ankle to a fountain in the courtyard of Valdivia's hacienda.

"Dr. Scarborough, I presume," Kyle had said with a jaunty lilt to his voice, though his eyes had scanned her with serious, almost startled interest—the same way she looked at him. They flirted outrageously, both trying to distract the other from the tense situation at hand, but Sara felt a deeper bond, one unlike anything she'd ever known before. Dinah stood nearby, silent, as if she knew that a special and private communion was taking place.

Kyle waited for Valdivia's wrath with fearless aplomb. He stood calmly in the sunny courtyard that day, a prisoner anticipating an ugly fate yet capable of offering reassurance to Sara. He was a hero beyond anything she'd ever imagined. At the last moment he took her hand, kissed it, and made her promise to name a plant after him—a perennial, he told her, with a big stem.

Her heart breaking, Sara hugged him and begged him to forgive her for being—even innocently—the cause of his predicament. He answered by drawing her into a fierce embrace, then kissing her. It was one of those moments that makes a small sanctuary in time, a mingling of heightened emotions and sensations that becomes an indelible memory, and she offered him everything in her soul.

Seconds later Valdivia walked into the courtyard. She told Valdivia that she'd do no more work on the herbicide if he harmed Kyle Surprise. Valdivia had simply smiled and pointed toward Dinah, who held her newborn baby, Katie. "You can protect one or the other," Valdivia said. "Either Mr. Surprise or Dinah's child. You choose."

As Dinah stiffened with horror and Sara took an outraged swing at Valdivia's jaw, Kyle shoved them both into the arms of Valdivia's men. "Sara chooses to protect the baby," he told Valdivia.

The men dragged her and Dinah to the edge of the courtyard.

"Stop," Valdivia ordered. "I want them to watch."

Sara struggled to free herself, but the guard's grip was too fierce. She stared at Kyle, and he raised one hand in farewell, his compelling gaze never leaving her. She screamed silently as a half dozen attack dogs were brought into the courtyard. Valdivia gave the command to kill.

She closed her eyes against the grisly scene that followed, but nothing could block the sounds of his anguish from her ears.

"I believe," Valdivia said to her and Dinah, "your friend has had enough."

She opened her eyes and cried out when she saw the guards dragging Kyle's body away, his blood smearing the white tiles of the courtyard.

"He is dead," Valdivia said.

Valdivia, thankfully, had lied. He'd kept Kyle a prisoner at another of his plantations until Kyle managed to recover enough to escape with the help of rebels. In the meantime Jeopard, his co-agent Drake Lancaster, and Dinah's husband, Rucker, infiltrated Valdivia's estate and carried out the rescue—but only because Kyle sent rebel troops to help.

Now those memories tormented Sara. Her eyes burning with affectionate tears, Sara watched the man on her video screen. He pulled a pair of jeans from a tote bag by his feet then unfastened his light trousers. He had his back to her, and her heart skipped as he slowly, very slowly, pushed the trousers down to reveal taut, angular hips covered in snug briefs.

The downward angle of the camera and the length of his shirttail prevented her from seeing as much as she would have liked. Sara felt lecherous when she realized that her breath was short with anticipation. But what was wrong with sneaking a peek? After all, he was on her land, provoking her against her wishes. And he was so beautiful, body and soul.

He bent over, easing the trousers down his legs. She could see ragged scars on the backs of his thighs, but they didn't dull the beauty of his powerful body. She thought of the roots of a magnificent tree she'd seen once in the Amazon river basin, roots that nature had molded into strong and lovely shapes. His rump flexed with muscle as he bent farther over, dropping the trousers to his ankles.

He straightened just as slowly, drawing his spread fingers up his legs until finally he rubbed them over his hips and, reaching under his shirt, snapped the waistband of his briefs with a jaunty flick of his thumbs. He kicked his running shoes off and stepped into the jeans.

Sara propped her chin on one hand and found herself sighing with pleasure as he bent over once again, tugging a pair of faded, rump-hugging denims into place. This man was dangerous. He'd confused her so much that she sat there growing warm and languid— while at the same time wanting to hit him for complicating her life.

He turned around and smoothed the palms of his hands over the bulge that his unzipped jeans outlined handsomely. Then he tucked in his Hawaiian shirt, zipped the jeans' zipper, smiled up into the camera as if he'd known all along that she was watching, *and blew her a kiss.*

Sara slammed backward into the chair, her mouth open. He'd discovered the security camera on the outside perimeter. Would he figure out that cameras were hidden in the trees all along the wall's quarter-mile path? Of course he would. And then what would he do?

He gave the camera a thumbs-up, then went to the ice chest and removed a small bottle full of dark liquid. He shook it, unscrewed the top, and raised the bottle in a salute. He reached into his tote bag again and retrieved some sort of hand tool. He put his running shoes back on and walked toward the camera, his gaze never wavering from the lens, one brow arched as if in rebuke.

When he stopped at the bottom edge of the camera's

range, he held the bottle up so that she could see it. A Coco-Moo chocolate drink. He seemed to consider it a symbol, a taunt of some kind. He disappeared from view under the camera, which was mounted in the upper limbs of an oak tree, and Sara gasped as she realized what he planned to do. Her video screen abruptly filled with gray static.

He had located the camera cable, and cut it.

Kyle spent the next two days exploring every foot of the wall. Sara watched her video screens in growing panic. Every time he found a camera he looked up into it and smiled wickedly at her.

Then he cut the cable.

He left only the camera at the gate unharmed. After he finished disconnecting the others, he pulled his ice chest in front of it, sat down, crossed his legs lazily, and pushed the intercom button. "Hello, Sara. I canceled your version of *Candid Camera*."

"You vandalized my property," she answered coldly. "I ought to call the sheriff and have you arrested."

"You won't." He grinned. "That would attract too much attention. Your privacy would be compromised. You might have to appear in public."

"I ought to open the gate and let my geese negotiate with you."

"Why not send the killer dogs? Or are there any killer dogs? I've been listening but I never hear a sound—not a growl, not a bark, nothing. I hear lots of geese honking, though. Have you trained your killer dogs to do geese impressions? Does *Star Search* know about this?"

Sara put her head in her hands. "Kyle, why don't you give up?"

"Because you owe me one."

"What?"

"You never named a plant after me." He crossed his

arms over a broad chest covered in a flannel shirt. "You promised."

"The perfect plant already has a name. *Kudzu*. It shows up where you least want it, makes itself very annoying, and takes over without any encouragement at all."

"All I want is a friendly visit with you. Just a few days. Give me a spot on the dungeon floor for my sleeping bag and I'll be happy. I won't ask about your research. I swear."

She shook her fists as if he could see them. "For months I was a prisoner living by rules I hated! Nobody will ever manipulate me again! The more you try, the more I'll say no!"

"Fear is controlling you. There's no reason to think that anyone would kidnap you again."

"That's not what I'm—" She caught herself. "Kyle, you hardly know me. I'm a loner. An oddball. Kids used to call me the 'mad scientist' when I was growing up. I graduated from high school when I was thirteen and got my bachelor's degree in biology when I was fifteen. By the time I was twenty I had my doctorate. Then I went to South America and spent years doing research by myself."

He nodded. "The summa cum laude bookworm. The genius. I read the agency report on you when I was assigned to find out why you'd disappeared. Do you know what else it said?"

"No."

"That you were a warm, outgoing person who always had a lot of friends. That you were devastated at fifteen when your father and brother died while working on a science project in the Arctic. That you and your mother were very close. In short, Doc, that you're very people-oriented."

"I've . . . changed," she said numbly. "I have to put my research first."

"Sara, open the gate and let me in. You don't have anything to be afraid of or to hide. What can the world take away from you?"

She couldn't tell him, so she turned both the intercom and the camera off. Immediately he rang the chime again, rang it repeatedly, as if angry and impatient. She ignored him.

Sara went to the crib she'd moved into a corner of the security room. Noelle lay there on her stomach, sleeping, her expression innocent and utterly trusting. Sara stroked her dark, almost black hair. What could the world take away?

"Everything," Sara whispered.

Once it became obvious that Kyle wouldn't give up the siege of Moonspell Keep, Sara was forced to consider new tactics. She called Tom and Lucy Wayne, the local couple who delivered her groceries once a week, and postponed their delivery for fear that Kyle would slip through the gate when she went to let them in. Tom tended the grounds and Lucy did some housekeeping, though only in the castle's main rooms, far away from Noelle's nursery and the lab.

Tom and Lucy had worked for her mother, and they were the only people Sara ever let inside the keep. Even they didn't know that she had a baby. She never asked them to deliver supplies for Noelle. Instead, she slipped out each month in her mother's old pickup truck, drove to a town thirty miles away, and bought a stock of formula, baby food, diapers, and anything else Noelle needed.

After calling the Waynes, Sara went outside to double-check the security systems around the castle. With the baby cuddled against her back in a soft canvas carrier and Daisy trailing at her heels, Sara scoured three acres of trees, shrubs, and flower beds, determined to make certain that nothing had been tampered with. She felt as if Kyle Surprise had invaded her inner sanctum already.

The geese—a dozen aggressively honking white birds of intimidating size and temperament—knew the second she set foot outdoors. They waddled up from their pond at the back of the estate, hissing at Daisy and eyeing Sara with greed. She set out their daily ration of cracked corn and watched them fight over it. They were vicious with any stranger who wandered into their territory, and, she knew from experience, their big blunt beaks could leave a nasty bruise.

You want a surprise, Mr. Surprise? Show your arrogant fanny to these feathered fiends.

Finally Sara went to the cobblestone yard and gazed up at her home. It was small, not a real castle, only twenty rooms, and all the upstairs ones had been closed off years before. There was only one turret and one pair of enormous chimneys. The tall, arched windows contained magnificent stained glass motifs that her grandfather had imported from his native England, but the security bars ruined the regal effect.

Marcus Scarborough had fancied himself the king of a small fiefdom. His daughter had been its princess. Sara smiled ruefully. His granddaughter was its sorceress, held here by a spell.

She crossed a heavy wooden bridge over a steep gully filled with painfully sharp privet hedge and stood in the castle's entranceway. Gazing across the front yard toward the massive gate in the distance, Sara wondered what Kyle was doing at his camp just outside, and when he would make his first attempt at scaling the walls.

She paced in the grand, arching entrance with its enormous door of hand-carved teak and felt even more threatened than she had before. Sara opened the door, pressed a button, and watched the bridge rise until it formed a barricade in front of the entrance. She was ready for him, and she was confident that he would not get inside her home the way he'd gotten inside her heart.

Exasperated and feeling none too gentle, Kyle decided that Sara reminded him of the tiny crabs that inhabited the marshes of his home state. When threatened, they ducked into their holes in the muddy sand, and nothing could tempt them out again. But a savvy spectator knew to wait, silent and calm. Marsh crabs were invariably too curious for their own good. Sara was a research scientist—like a crab, curiosity was a force she couldn't resist.

So Kyle counted the days and waited for her to come out.

Exactly one week after his siege began, on an overcast afternoon that smelled of cool rain and woodsmoke from his campfire, Kyle looked up from the spy thriller he was laughing over—he wished that the real world were as neat and simple—to listen as distant footsteps crunched on dried leaves. Sara appeared in the woods at the point where the stone wall made a sharp bend to the right.

Kyle watched her stride toward his camp, her eyes locked on him, her hands jammed defensively into the pockets of white overalls that she wore with a pink sweatshirt. Pink and white were perfect colors for her; in them she stood out like a butterfly in the somber surroundings.

He stood up slowly, angled a leg out to one side, hooked his thumbs into the belt loops of his jeans, and tried to appear relaxed. Pleasure and frustration made a knot in his stomach. Before the incident in Surador he'd had an easy way with women, women of all shapes, sizes, ages, and cultures. His far-flung work had given him ample opportunity for variety. He liked women, inside and out, intellect and curves, the whole package. And, before the scars, they had liked him.

He was tormented by his need for Sara—lovely, unique, and kind-hearted despite her stubborn refusal to let him inside her private Camelot. She was utterly determined to pretend that he didn't resemble the lead character in a horror flick. Freddy. Jason. Kyle. Maybe he had a movie career ahead of him.

She looked at him stoically as she came to a stop on the opposite side of his campfire. Her face was more unusual than pretty, the face of a sloe-eyed forest elf, the queen of the elves, in fact—with a regal jut to the chin and green eyes full of dignity. The image needed only to be framed by a pair of delicately pointed ears to make it mythical.

Kyle couldn't help letting his gaze trace the contours of a voluptuous mouth that belonged in a men's magazine ad cooing something about fast cars, warm nights, and irresistible aftershave. Right now there wasn't a coo within a mile of that mouth.

"This is ridiculous," she told him firmly.

"That's right, Tinker Bell."

"I have some shopping to do. I can put it off only for another couple of days."

"You mean you actually venture into the big bad world?"

"On occasion." She raised her chin defiantly. "See? I'm not a complete recluse. You can stop worrying about me and go home."

He gestured at her unprotected surroundings. "Aren't you afraid to be out here with me? There might be dragons, and I'm no Sir Lancelot."

She looked at him pensively. "I remember a time when you were."

His chest constricted on an aching sensation of loss,

of chances stolen, of a time when he could have charmed her, won her. "Long gone," he muttered.

"No. A scarred knight is still a knight. Still noble." She paused. "But misguided. This damsel isn't in distress."

"Then let me see for myself." He jerked his thumb toward the gate. "Open it."

"No."

His patience evaporated. "Then why the hell did you come out here to talk?"

"You want to visit with me! So visit!" She held out her arms. "I'm trying to compromise! Here I am! Do what you want!"

Drops of cold rain whipped through the trees, the heralds of a deluge that began five seconds later. "Visit accepted," Kyle said loudly. He grabbed her hand and pulled her to his tent, a low, dome-shaped structure meant for a solitary occupant or two very well-acquainted ones.

They sat down cross-legged on his rumpled sleeping bag atop the soft cushion of an air mattress, while the rain beat a loud tattoo on the material overhead. Sara's damp hair and clothes filled his senses with a pleasant feminine smell that included a light fragrance, whether perfume or simply the result of her work with flowers, he didn't know. Her hand lay cool and tense inside his grip, but she didn't pull away.

She looked around, her cheeks flushed as if she were trying to avoid his eyes. His flowered shirt was neatly folded atop his tote bag. She pointed at it. "I think you've got some Circaea Quadrisulcata there."

"Don't insult me in Latin," he ordered mildly.

"The small white flowers on your shirt. They look like Circaea Quadrisulcata. Enchanters' nightshade. A pretentious name originally assigned to a more interesting plant, according to mythology, by the Greek enchantress, Circe."

"Isn't nightshade dangerous?"

"Not this one. It isn't part of the same family. The name's not related."

"So." He smiled sardonically. "What does my taste in shirts say about me? That I'm a fake enchanter and not dangerous?"

Sara pushed dewy red hair off her forehead. "Hardly!"

"Which part? Both? I am dangerous? I am an enchanter?"

"You are a smooth talker who could probably charm the Zonotrichia Albicolli down from the deciduous perennials."

"Birds from the trees?" he guessed.

She nodded. "Very good."

"Then why can't I charm you out of your fortress?"

"You did. I'm here."

"For how long?"

She looked at a man's digital wristwatch mounted on a thick silver stretch band. "Fifteen minutes."

"Yow! An eternity. What's with the man's watch?"

She held her small-boned wrist up so that he could see the watch's complex dial. "I use the stopwatch in my lab work. I couldn't find a woman's watch that had all the features I wanted."

"Speaking of timing and relationships, tell me the approximate date of your last social outing with a man."

"I beg your pardon?"

He arched a brow. "A *datus Friday-nightus*. A big date."

She scowled at him, and deep wariness glimmered in her eyes. Her fingers stiffened even more inside his grip. "I'm not lonely."

"Any prospects?"

"Not lately."

"Not since before the . . . before Surador?"

She looked embarrassed. "Right." More than embarrassed. Worried. Evasive. She began trying to tug her hand away from his.

Kyle suddenly realized that his interrogation must sound like a come-on. His scars seemed to burn his skin; he was acutely aware of each one. He let go of her hand and said as lightly as he could, "Hey, I'm not hinting for personal reasons, all right? I just want some straight answers about your happiness."

Her eyes locked on his with an intensity that made him feel vulnerable. She searched them while he cursed silently, but couldn't look away. Her expression softened. "So when was your last datus Friday-nightus, Mr. Surprise?"

"Oh, no, Doc, you're not turning the tables on me. I'm an expert at interrogation."

"Uhmmm. A definite lack of social activity, I suspect. How interesting. Perhaps you and I are both hermits, only in different ways."

"I haven't walled myself—"

"What are *you* afraid of, Kyle?" The victorious gleam in her eye began to annoy him. "You enjoy baiting me, patronizing me—"

"Maybe, but it's for your own good. And I told you up front that helping you would help me—"

"How? What are you trying to prove to yourself? Are you so afraid you have nothing to offer a woman that you have to prove that you do, even if it's only by playing therapist?"

Months of hidden frustration and self-doubt boiled over. Wounded right down to his carefully nourished sense of truth, Kyle grabbed her by the shoulders and cursed softly. "See for yourself what I can still offer."

She murmured an anguished litany as he lowered his mouth to hers. "Don't. Can't. Shouldn't . . ." But then he was kissing her, moving his lips over hers in a seductive challenge, putting every skill he possessed into the kiss as he tried to strip away time and bad memories and scars, both his and hers.

Sara knotted her fists into his flannel shirt and jerked fiercely, but at the same time she kept her mouth against his and received the thrust of his tongue without resisting. Angry, trembling, she slipped her tongue forward and stroked in return. Kyle groaned and heard her answering plea—for mercy, but also for more.

For one magnificent second he tasted the sweetness and heat he had so often dreamed about, the welcome that he had hoped to provoke in her regardless of his appearance. They shared the culmination of fantasies and promises that needed to be kept. But she drew back, half crying, looked at him with a grimace of regret, and turned her head as if she couldn't stand his ravaged face.

He was speechless for a moment, while his exhilaration drained away and a hollow feeling replaced it. "I guess I settled two doubts at once," he said finally. "I've still got plenty to offer, but you'd rather I didn't offer again."

She nodded at him wearily, her head bowed. "I'm so sorry it has to be this way."

Kyle's emotions hardened into a fist inside his chest. "Don't feel embarrassed. Not long after I came home from Surador a few of my old acquaintances dropped in to visit. They tried to act cheerful, but . . . Sara, you're not the first woman who couldn't quite hide her reaction to my scars. Don't blame yourself."

Her head jerked up. Her eyes glittered with shock. "You think that's why I stopped kissing you?" When he nodded, sorrow and regret filled her eyes. "Oh, Kyle, no."

He stiffened in amazement as she took his face between her hands and quickly brushed her lips over several of the larger scars. She pulled away from him, shaking her head when he leaned forward again. "No. No more. I mean it, Kyle."

Bewildered and desperate for answers, he frowned at her. "What do you need, Sara? What do you want?"

"Nothing. I'm doing okay," she said with deliberate vagueness. "You can't change my life-style. Someday I'll change it myself, but not now." She glanced at her wristwatch. "Now I have to go. This is the last time I'll see you. I mean it. God bless you, Kyle. I wish things were easier to explain. Good-bye."

She tried to rise to her feet, but he trapped her wrist with a firm grip. Breathing raggedly, Kyle shook his head. "Go into town with me. Have dinner. At least do that much."

"I can't."

He slid around so that he blocked the exit from the tent. "Then you can stay and talk. There's no reason for you to hurry back to the castle."

"Experiments," she said, staring at him anxiously.

He uttered a cheerful but earthy opinion of her bluff. "I won't kiss you again. I promise. Relax."

"Please. Let me go."

"I'm holding you prisoner for the rest of the afternoon." He gestured around them at the tent's brightly colored walls. "It's not an ugly dungeon. And I don't intend to torture you." He inhaled with a great show of contentment. "Enjoy the sound of the rain. Take your shoes off. Unbuckle that AM-FM-clock-radio-toaster-oven around your wrist."

She curled her legs under her and sat on her heels, her hands clasped on her lap. For a second Kyle had the disturbing notion that she was about to beg for her freedom. "I really did leave a delicate . . . experiment. I don't want it to be alone for more than a few minutes."

"Sara, you can't make me believe that a bunch of *plants* need your constant attention."

"You make it sound as if I'm growing petunias for my

patio. I'm talking about sophisticated laboratory projects."

"All right. You can leave. I'll go with you."

"No!" She ground the word out angrily. "I've visited with you, which is what you said you wanted! I've told you over and over that I'm happy, that I want to be left alone, that I will *never* let you inside my home! What is it going to take to make you believe me?"

Kyle leveled calm eyes on her. "I don't believe that you're happy any more than I believe that you want to be left alone. I *do* believe that you have to be forced back into the world."

She leaned toward him, her expression fierce. "I don't want to hurt you. I never want to see anything bad happen to you again. But I have to tell you something." She took a calming breath. "I left a recording on my phone system. It says that an armed man has vandalized my cameras and is now trying to break into my estate." She glanced at her watch. "If I don't get back soon, that recording, complete with my address, is going straight to the county sheriff's office. When he comes to arrest you, I'll add attempted kidnapping and assault to the charges. And I *will* file charges."

Kyle had to admire her tenacity and resourcefulness. She had a brilliant, stubborn, mysterious mind, and she was a challenge worthy of every skill he possessed. He silently declared war on her. A gentle kind of war, but one without retreat.

"What are you so desperate to protect, Sara?"

She thumped a fist against her leg. "Myself! My sanity! Now let me go!"

He nodded and moved aside. "I'll be leaving as soon as the rain stops."

She froze, gazing at him with shock and, he noted happily, a certain amount of wistfulness. "Really?"

"Really. I've done all I can do. I'll send someone to repair all the camera cables."

Her watch began to beep. "Three-minute warning," she said, distracted and frowning. "I have to hurry."

"Good-bye, Tinker Bell. Take care of yourself." He smiled with just the right degree of stoic cheer. "That was a great kiss. Thanks for making me feel better than I have in a long time."

The tent wasn't tall enough for standing. She crawled to the door and halted, warily watching him. The lonely, almost tragic expression that washed over her face tore at his belly just as the lie about leaving had.

She pressed her fingertips to her lips, kissed them, then brushed them over his mouth. "I'll never forget you," she murmured. She scrambled out of the tent.

Kyle slipped outside and stood in the drenching rain, watching until she disappeared around the curve in the wall. Then he began to pack. And make war plans.

Three

Sara waited until the next morning and then decided to see if Kyle had made good on his intention to go home. She left Noelle sleeping in the safe confines of her crib and went down a long staircase into the castle's cellar. The steel door in its far wall opened when she punched a code into the electronic lock.

Sara entered her underground greenhouse, a cavern of chiseled rock walls that could easily accommodate a thousand tropical plants. Besides one large main area, it was divided into a dozen self-contained glass cubicles, each with separate light, temperature, and moisture controls for different plant needs and experiments.

In the open space colorful seedlings from dozens of species grew in trays set on neat rows of tables. Candy-colored butterflies fluttered through the cavern, crickets sang in the shadows, and several pairs of small parrots talked noisily from their perches in a small tree.

Sara inhaled ripe, humid air and felt the heat radiated by a rock ceiling covered with fluorescent lights. An underground cavern was not the ideal place for a tropical greenhouse, obviously, but her mother had spent years developing it, and it served its purpose well.

Exiting through another steel door on the far side of the cavern, she entered a low, narrow corridor of claustrophobic dimensions, lit by tiny white lights at head level on the walls. The air became cool and musty; she felt smothered in a way that she never did ordinarily. Sara rubbed a palm over the taut muscles in the back of her neck, lifting feathery red hair.

Kyle had reminded her of all she was missing, all she'd given up to protect Noelle from unwanted questions and scrutiny. Now she felt like a plant reaching desperately for sunlight that could never be hers. For the first time since her return from Surador she found herself chafing under the restrictions of her reclusive life, even while she knew she'd make the same choices again.

Sara climbed a narrow set of stone steps to a landing just wide enough for her to stand easily. The stairs proceded upward for another dozen yards, their angle gradually growing so shallow that they were hardly stairs anymore. Near the top their smooth surfaces were strewn with decaying leaves. The stairs ended at a double door that lay flat above them, at ground level.

Sara pushed a lever on a control panel set in the landing wall, and the doors opened upward with a soft whirring sound. Golden maple leaves floated into the stairwell; bright sunlight poured down, so warm and friendly that she thought of Kyle again and fought off feelings of sorrow.

After she climbed out of the passageway and stood in the crisp autumn morning, surrounded by forest, she closed the doors with a remote-control unit. She hung the device on the elastic waistband of her white sweat pants and carefully tugged the tail of her matching top over it.

Then she slipped through the woods as quietly as

she could. But Kyle was gone and his camping site was already obscured by a covering of newly fallen leaves. Her shoulders stiffened with unhappy satisfaction. Sara went to the empty area and stood, gazing bleakly about. He had even scattered the rocks that had circled his fire.

A thoughtful camper, that was Kyle. Don Johnson playing Sonny Crockett pretending to be a Boy Scout, with a kissing technique worth a dozen merit badges. She wanted him, she needed him, but drawing him into her life would be the cruelest thing she could do.

The forest seemed more quiet than usual, and the autumn breeze made a forlorn, empty sound in the highest tree branches. Tears blurred her vision. Sara picked a leaf up and let it go, watching it spiral, caught in forces it couldn't control.

Diego de Valdivia, the power-hungry man who had forced her participation in an immoral type of research, the South American business *patrón* who had secretly dabbled in espionage, the man who had maimed Kyle forever, was Noelle's father.

Kyle gave her two days in which to relax and grow careless. Shortly after midnight of the second day he left his motel room and drove back to her estate, hid his rental car in the woods near her driveway, and set out through the dark forest on foot, carrying a backpack full of gear. He kept clear of the gate at the main road to avoid setting off the sensors he knew were hidden there.

He ruefully eyed the dragons that snarled in a sliver of moonlight atop the gate's massive pillars. Her dragons were friendly, she'd said. Sure. And so were his nightmares.

When he reached the walls around the keep he went straight to an oak tree he'd scouted out the week before. From his pack Kyle pulled a grappling hook with a rope attached to it. He threw the hook over one of the oak's thick, outflung limbs.

Still wearing the backpack, he climbed fifty feet of rope hand over hand, using muscles that burned with protest because he hadn't indulged in such a feat since his days at the Naval Academy, fifteen years earlier. Kyle sat on the tree limb for a few minutes, catching his breath.

He was high above the keep's wall, and in the distance the castle's dark, ghostly visage shone clearly. It was a small but very authentic-looking medieval fortress, he discovered. He wouldn't have been shocked to see knights riding up in a procession as a princess waved from an upper window.

Goose bumps rose on Kyle's arms as he coiled his rope and fixed the grappling hook for another toss. He threw it at a sturdy-looking walnut tree not far inside the grounds. After he'd secured a taut line of rope from one tree to the other, Kyle wrapped his arms and legs around it and edged over the wall, many feet below.

When he was safely ensconced in the walnut tree he pulled a nightvision scope from his pack and gazed through it, studying the neatly kept gardens for any sign of dogs, geese—or dragons. None, he thought in grim victory. He'd bet a year's supply of Coco-Moos that there were no dogs, the geese were harmless, and as for the dragons, well, he'd take his chances.

From the walnut tree he tossed a rope to the roof of the castle. The roof was flat and had battlements, much to his amusement. The grappling hook clattered into one of their narrow gaps and wedged snugly. Kyle crossed his last rope bridge. By morning he would find a way inside the keep. Victory.

Daisy was *not* a nervous dog. In fact, Sara suspected that her nerve endings were coated with marshmallow.

That was why her behavior in front of the fireplace puzzled Sara so much. As Sara sipped her morning coffee she watched the dog stand with head cocked, growling softly, chocolate-brown eyes trained on the giant opening. The fireplace was the focal point of the castle's main room, a two-story chamber braced by thick wood beams and decorated with an assortment of plush leather furniture, tapestries, bookcases, and luxurious rugs.

The hearth could have served as a small dance floor; the firebox itself was taller than Sara's head and so deep that all five feet two inches of her could lie down in it. Sara had to stand on a kitchen stool to reach the stone mantel, and dusting the Scarborough family crest that hung over the mantel required a stepladder.

She lounged in the kitchen doorway, where she could keep one eye on Daisy and one on Noelle, who was gurgling happily in her high chair as she flung baby food on the kitchen floor. At ten months, eating was one of Noelle's supreme entertainments.

"What is it?" Sara asked the dog.

Daisy fluffed her golden jowls in a soft woof. She walked to the logs stacked on lion's-head andirons and tried to peer up the chimney. She growled again. Sara listened intently and finally heard small scuffing and scratching sounds. She sighed with relief.

"It's just another owl," she told Daisy. "Just some little bitty owl who got in under the chimney cap. It'll find its way out eventually."

She went back to Noelle, who had gleefully turned her plastic cup upside down so that remnants of orange juice trickled out of the spout onto her lap, the high chair, and the floor. "Mop!" she said clearly, smiling up at her mother.

"Mom," Sara corrected her, gently wiping her hands with a cloth.

In Noelle's lingo *mop* was not something with which

one cleaned up baby food several times a day, it was the person who did the cleaning. Noelle made smacking sounds and pursed her mouth. Sara laughed at that signal, while her chest filled with a warm feeling of contentment. Bending over, she took Noelle's face between her hands and kissed her lightly, tasting orange juice, formula, and scrambled eggs. "I love you too. Time for our bath, breakfast-lips."

She carried Noelle through the main room, where Daisy still listened at the fireplace, her ears pricked. "We're going to take a bath, Daisy Doolittle." Sara knew that nothing would keep Noelle's canine pal from following them from the room.

But Daisy didn't budge. Noelle called "Zee, Zee"—her version of Daisy's name—but the dog ignored even that. Finally Sara had to drag Daisy from the room by the scruff of the neck and shut the door behind her.

He did *not* feel like Santa Claus.

Kyle let himself down stone by stone, his toes aching inside his running shoes from constantly fighting for a hold on the slick wall. The chimney was suffocating, full of the soot and smell left by thousands of fires. When he looked up he saw blue sky. When he looked down he saw darkness, followed by a stone ledge, an open damper, and a glimmer of light.

Victory.

A few minutes later Kyle eased out of the fireplace and stood gazing at a majestic room outfitted in a style that was very English and very appealing—old brass lamps, stained-glass windows that would have done justice to a cathedral, and plush leather furniture with a comfortable, well-worn look.

He glanced down at his blackened clothes and skin. Santa Claus never had to deal with soot, apparently. Moving on silent, careful feet, Kyle explored. Off the main room was a cheerful blue kitchen with modern appliances. Gingham curtains decorated a sunny bay window. The window was barred on the outside. The kitchen was connected via a short hall to a dining room that rivaled the big den for splendor and size.

Going back past the fireplace, Kyle opened a heavy paneled door and stepped into an arching hallway with a carpeted floor. He tilted his head toward the faint sound of water running. After a second he decided that someone was emptying a tub, not filling it. Along the hallway he discovered guest rooms and an alcove at the end with a double door that suggested a master suite. Kyle tested an ornate silver doorknob there. It turned easily, and he slowly drew the door open.

A snarl greeted him. Hackles rose in a shaggy golden ruff. White fangs shown under curled lips.

Kyle's breath caught. This dog was no trained guard animal—it was a mishmash of unimpressive, ill-fitting parts, and he doubted that it weighed more than forty pounds—but it meant business. Bitter, deeply lodged memories flared to life. He would never let a dog bite him again.

He pulled his pistol and aimed for a point right between the animal's eyes. If it made one step toward him, he'd shoot. *Hi, Tinker Bell. Didn't mean to upset you. I just did a Santa act down your chimney. Then I killed your pooch. Ho, ho, ho.* Kyle lowered the pistol but didn't remove his finger from the trigger.

At the same time, he swept his gaze around a bright, contemporary bedroom done in pretty pastels—nothing like the other rooms, with their dark, ornate furniture and stone floors. Through an open door across the master suite Kyle saw a large bathroom. The blue-tiled floor was wet; a thick white towel was jumbled on the side of a blue tub. He turned his attention back to the bedroom, studying the door that stood open in the wall to his left.

Kyle gave it puzzled scrutiny. It wasn't an ordinary door. For one thing, it was too narrow. He would have had to turn his broad shoulders sideways to fit them through the frame. The door hinged on the left side, so that it opened toward him, and he couldn't see what lay beyond it. Not yet, anyway. He would.

"Back, mutt," Kyle told the lanky dog. He made his voice very kind and complimentary. "You're the ugliest damned dog I've ever seen. You've got splayed feet and a pigeon chest. If your eyes were any closer together, you'd look like a cyclops. I hate dogs."

The snarl faded a little. The tip of a bushy tail wagged.

"You're stupid too," Kyle said sweetly. He eased a hand forward. "Make friends, potato-head." A salvo of barking poured from the dog's throat. Kyle jerked his hand back and pointed the gun again. He heard footsteps scuffing softly on a carpeted surface beyond the odd-looking door.

"Daisy, *what* is your problem?" Sara pushed the door open and peered around it. She gasped audibly when she saw Kyle, and both hands went to her throat in a protective gesture. "Oh, no, *no!*"

"Call 'Daisy,' " he said as calmly as he could, considering that "Daisy" looked as if she were ready to do a pit-bull impression.

"Don't shoot her!" Sara bolted into the room, hurriedly locked the strange door by entering a code into a small box beneath the doorknob, then ran to Daisy and knelt beside her. She wrapped both arms around Daisy's neck and gazed up at Kyle in speechless dismay.

He gazed back with an equal amount of discomfort. The short, sheer robe she wore was a shade of green that intensified the green of her eyes. It was tightly belted around her waist, which made the top gape, revealing an expanse of fair skin and the inner curves of small, perfectly formed breasts.

She'd somehow managed to splash water all over the

front of the robe, and it clung to her breasts and belly in breathtaking detail. Her face was flushed from the heat of the bathroom, and her damp hair lay in pretty wisps along the edges of her face. An incredibly provocative elf glared up at him.

"Get out! Damn you! You lied to me! Get out!"

"I'll be waiting," Kyle informed her. He let his eyes roam over her in a nonchalant way as he backed out the door. "In the great room."

"Get out!"

He bowed like an old-world gallant, then stepped into the hall and swung the bedroom door shut.

Distracted and afraid, Sara checked and double-checked the lock on Noelle's nursery door. The nursery, her laboratory, and the security room were all on the back side of the keep's main level, with the bedrooms, great room, kitchen, and dining room on the front, though a secret hallway connected Sara's bedroom to the nursery. She had come down that hallway when she heard Daisy bark.

Sara hurriedly dressed in jeans and a sweatshirt, then headed for the great room. Kyle had deceived her; worse than that, he now threatened the sanctuary that she'd spent the past nineteen months building to protect the secret she intended to keep at all costs. What kind of man would continue harassing her with such single-minded devotion?

One who thinks he's doing it for your own good, she admitted silently.

He stood in the great room, rubbing a wet kitchen towel over his sooty face. The gold and copper tapestry of his hair was a grimy mess; his shoes, jeans, flannel shirt, and jacket looked as if they'd never be the same. "I came down the chimney," he explained. "Merry Christmas."

"My unwanted chimney sweep," she said grimly, clenching her fists. "Why? Give me a reasonable excuse."

"None available, except that I'm a mean bastard at heart. I want to make you miserable—so miserable that you'll run like hell right back to the real world."

"I'm definitely miserable. But I'm not leaving this place. And you're not staying."

"I can't go back the way I came. A dragon spooked my reindeer. I'll have to catch the next sleigh, and I don't have a sleigh schedule."

She groaned with frustration. "Stop trying to make a joke out of this!"

"I won't be a problem guest. Tell me what's off limits and I'll stay out of it. I swear."

"I don't trust you. I tried to already. In return you broke into my home, sneaked into my bedroom, and threatened my dog."

"I wouldn't have shot that genetic reject. I mean it. I can't make any promises about defending myself from the vicious rottweilers, though." He glanced around coyly. "Where are they?"

Sara sank into a chair and put her head in her hands. "There aren't any attack dogs."

"That was a pretty nasty deception you used on me, Sara."

"I know. I suppose we're even, then."

"All right. Even." He came to her and squatted beside her knees.

"This is an impossible situation," she muttered.

"Have a little faith. I'm not going to hurt you or anything you care about." His tone filled with disgust. "We beat Valdivia, you know. He didn't get to sell your research the way he'd intended, he was exposed and shamed in a way that ruined him, and he killed himself because of it." Kyle took her hands. "But if you and I still let him control our lives, then he won. He got the last laugh. I hate the S.O.B. and everything he created. *I won't let him win.*"

Sara stared at him numbly. *I hate the S.O.B. and everything he created.* Would that include Noelle? If she'd had any hope that Kyle could accept her child, it withered. Who could believe that she loved a child who had been conceived in fear and hatred? Noelle must never be hurt by the stigma of Valdivia's legacy, and Kyle must never be hurt by what would surely look like an ugly betrayal of everything he had sacrificed.

Sara met his eyes and was nearly hypnotized by the way the vibrant blue stood out against the grime on his face. The concern and sincerity in his gaze made her want to scream with frustration. She could happily spend the rest of her life looking into those eyes. "You don't know what you're asking from me."

"Just friendship. Just trust."

"Just."

He smiled wearily. "We both know how rare those things are in the world."

"You absolutely won't leave. I'd have to call the sheriff to drag you off. And you know I won't do that."

He shrugged, managing to look both remorseful and pleased. "I swear I won't go anywhere except where you give permission. I swear." He took her hand and brought the fingertips to one of the harsh white ridges that zigzagged across his cheek. "I swear on these," he said gruffly.

Sara shivered inside. She was trapped. She could either play along or tell him the truth. Maybe, just maybe she could keep Noelle hidden from him.

"I . . . I won't have much free time," she warned. "I have crucial work to do in the lab. I can't be away from it for very long." She began to plan how she was going to heat baby food over a Bunsen burner.

"I'll be a terrific guest. I can cook," he announced abruptly. "Do you like chili?"

"I suppose . . . yes." Every nerve in her body felt the slow, soothing stroke of his fingers in her palm. "How long did you hide on my roof?"

"Six or seven hours. It took me that long to remove the stone chimney cap."

"Your determination is amazing."

He grinned. "You ain't seen nothing yet."

"Don't get overconfident. I have to do some shopping today. You can't come with me. And don't ask questions about it."

"All right." He thought for a second. "Do you play cards?" She nodded fervently. "Poker?" he asked.

"Oh, yes! It's been so long! I've missed it so much!"

"What else have you missed?" He looked at her closely, his eyes searching. Sara's breath stalled as she wondered what he was going to suggest next. It hurt so much to know that she couldn't encourage anything more than friendship.

Kyle, I'd like you to meet my daughter. The man who scarred you for life is her father. Do you think you can forgive and forget?

She didn't know how she was going to go shopping for her monthly baby supplies without him discovering Noelle. She couldn't leave the baby untended. Sara trembled inside and struggled for a plan.

"What have you missed the most?" Kyle persisted.

"I like to talk," she told him dully. "That's one of the things I've missed. Conversation."

A wide, handsome smile slid across his mouth. "I knew my tongue would come in handy here."

"Bite it," she instructed, lifting one reddish brow.

"Whatever you say," he agreed. "Your wish is my command, fair lady."

If only it were that simple. Sara wondered how she was going to resist the temptation.

She had to admit that it was exciting to sit in the kitchen with another adult, even a dangerous one. Kyle's presence created strange responses in her overwrought senses, but at the same time soothed her. She watched the graceful masculine strength of his hands as they curled around a pottery mug; she found her thoughts wandering in abstract ways. The lip of her own mug suddenly had textures she'd never noticed before, and when she drew her mouth over it she remembered every nuance of his kiss.

"Here are the rules," she told him. "If you follow the main hall past my bedroom, you'll see that it ends at a set of security doors." She smiled grimly. "They're built of two-inch steel plate, they're wired with alarms, and they unlock only on a voice command—mine. Don't ever try to get past those doors."

"That's where your lab is?"

"Yes." *And Noelle's nursery.*

"It's a deal."

"The front side of the keep is yours to use as you want. Pick whichever of the guest rooms suits you best." Sara looked up at him and managed a smile. "I hope you appreciate the combination of medieval decor and modern central heating."

"After tents and a cheap motel, it'll be great."

"I suppose you need to go back to the motel to get your clothes and things."

"Yes." He took a swig of coffee and swallowed deeply.

Sara was intrigued by the silky flexing of muscles in his throat. She quickly dropped her gaze to the open collar of his filthy shirt, but found herself admiring the curly, dark blond chest hair it revealed.

"Can you drop me off at my car when you go shopping?" he asked. "I left it near the main road."

Sara rubbed her forehead and tried to hide her distress. This was going to be more complicated than she'd thought. She had to go buy baby supplies; she had to take Noelle with her. All without him noticing. "Okay," she answered, frowning.

"You need to tell me how to open the gate and get

back into the castle without using the chimney. Don't look so worried about it," he urged, sounding puzzled and a little impatient. "Just what do you think I'm going to do—sabotage your research? Spy on you and report back to my old cronies? I'm *retired*, Tinker Bell."

"I'm sorry if I appear paranoid. It's just that I'm afraid that the government will always be curious about my new projects."

"If they're watching, they're not going to interfere with your life."

Her head snapped up. She shoved her coffee cup away, stood, and went to the bay window. The window seat was decorated with throw pillows covered in her mother's crochet. Sara snatched one into her arms and hugged it as she stared blindly out the window. Kyle rose and came over to her. She quivered when his hands cupped her shoulders from behind.

"You're really terrified of being under surveillance?" he asked gently.

"Yes. I get mental images of swarthy guys in trench coats hanging around outside my gate."

"Nah." He stroked her arms. "I feel certain that no one is watching you in person. Besides, if our people keep an eye on you, it's only to make sure no unfriendly types ever get a chance to coerce you again."

Sara hugged the pillow harder. "Our government has its own schemes and needs," she said. "I'm not certain if they're any better than the rest." What if the government busybodies found out about Noelle? It would be easy to estimate her birth month and determine that she'd been conceived right before the rescue in Surador, that her father had been one of the black-haired, olive-skinned nationalists of Spanish descent.

Sara couldn't help shivering. What if that discovery led to the truth about her and Valdivia? Would she be accused of aiding him? Could the authorities take Noelle away from her, or use the baby to force her into the kind of research she'd sworn never to do again?

"Tinker Bell, I didn't mean to upset you."

She whipped around and searched his face. "You have inside information. *Am* I being watched?"

"Not closely, I imagine. Remember, I'm retired. I'm not cleared to receive information on current operations. But no one from our side is going to bother you. You've watched too many silly espionage movies. The real world is not full of spies and devious plans. It's pretty straightforward most of the time."

"I don't think I'll ever feel completely safe again," she whispered hoarsely. "I used to be so overconfident. I thought I was smarter and tougher and more independent than everybody else. I roamed all over South America planning ways to save the world with biology." She made a derisive sound. "The great Dr. Scarborough—young, brilliant, wealthy, pretty—so stupid when it came to judging human nature that she couldn't tell when she was getting into deep trouble."

"Valdivia was a chameleon," Kyle said bitterly. "For a long time we thought he was just another aristocratic *patrón*, with an eye for luxury and a way of charming everyone he met. So he fooled us too."

He pulled her to him and held her tightly. Sara dropped the pillow and wrapped her arms around his waist. She cried out sadly because his comfort and strength were a torment, a gift she could never keep.

"Shhh," he crooned. "If I were James Bond, I'd know exactly what to do next. I'd say something cocky and suave, like 'I have a lovely little villa on the Mediterranean, where the sun is warm and the champagne is cold and the nights are very, very hot. Come away with me, my beautiful, sad Dr. Scarborough. There's a wonderful view of the ocean from the villa's master bedroom.'"

Sara's senses whirled; reckless need sang in her blood. She loved the feel of his chest hair tickling her cheek. His torso pressed closer to hers, and his thighs parted slightly, inviting hers to nestle between them. All it would take to feel him resting intimately against her belly would be a subtle roll of her hips.

"If this were a James Bond film," Sara said weakly, "I'd be wearing something much sexier than a floppy gray sweatshirt and jeans, and I'd have a much bigger bosom. I'd lick my overglossed lips and say with just the right amount of kittenish sophistication, 'Oh, Mr. Bond, I'd love to see your waves crest.' "

He threw his head back and laughed. Sara looked up and enjoyed the white flash of his teeth and the way laugh lines gave his face a wickedly mischievous expression. The harshness of the scars couldn't dim the sheer joy in this man. It lay under the surface like a spring that nourished every bit of life that came near it.

But his laughter died when he looked down and noticed her scrutinizing his savage features. "Daydreams," he said with a grunt of dismay. "They're harmless." He stepped back abruptly. "You're going shopping? I'll make you a grocery list. You can bring back the ingredients for Surprise chili."

"Abracadabra. It will be provided." Feeling awkward and emotional, Sara covered by making a comical curtsy. "The sorceress of Moonspell Keep, at your service. Spells cast, potions mixed, wicked enchantments broken."

"Can you turn a frog into a prince?" he asked with grim humor that bore no trace of self-pity.

Sara studied him for a moment, wanting so much to help that she momentarily forgot all her worries. "It should be easy. I like frogs *and* princes. I'll see what I can do."

He nodded. "Deal."

Sara gazed at him solemnly. "Deal."

Four

Sara smoothed the soft collar of Noelle's pink snowsuit.
"Stay quiet, little bunny," she whispered to the baby.
"Just until I get you to the truck." Noelle's black lashes
fluttered but her eyes remained closed. The pacifier in
her mouth wiggled up and down with each movement
of her mouth. She was utterly trusting and innocent.
She was also, thank goodness, sound asleep. Looking
at her restored Sara's confidence. She closed the top of
the wicker picnic basket in which the baby slept.

All she had to do was keep Noelle out of sight until
she dropped Kyle off at the end of the driveway, where
he'd left his car. It would be a ten-minute ordeal, no
more. Sara couldn't think of a reasonable excuse for
refusing him a ride. Besides, his quiet scrutiny un-
nerved her, and she didn't want to provoke any more
questions than she could help.

Her plan was simple. The pickup truck had a camper
hood. Curtains covered all the windows. During the
past hour Sara had carefully secured the curtains with
masking tape, so there'd be no chance of Kyle catching
a glimpse between them. With a length of heavy rope
she had fastened Noelle's car seat in one corner of the

truck bed. After they were safely away from Kyle, Sara would move the baby to the front seat. The day was sunny; the camper's interior was pleasantly warm. Noelle would be comfortable and Daisy would keep her company. Ten minutes. That was all Sara needed.

The picnic basket was larger than average and Noelle was smaller. The basket had survived years of Scarborough family outings. Sara smiled wistfully, remembering. With two biologists for parents and two aspiring biologists for children, the picnics had often turned into field trips. This basket had held potato salad and birds' nests, fried chicken and snakeskins.

And now it held a precious secret.

Her hands trembling with nervousness, she hooked the strap of a floppy leather purse over one shoulder, then lifted the basket slowly, her palms sweating on the wide wooden handles. If she could get through this month's shopping trip safely, the rest of Kyle's visit shouldn't pose too many problems.

"Come on, Daisy. Let's just keep our cool and act like nothing's odd."

Daisy trotted out of the bedroom in front of Sara. Sara eased the basket to the hallway floor, then shut and locked the bedroom door. Her pulse thready, she carried the basket down the hall and stopped outside a door to one of the guest rooms.

Kyle's odd surname was derived from the more elegant-sounding St. Surpris. She remembered someone telling her that Kyle's great-great-grandfather was a French pirate who settled in Florida. Considering the way Kyle had come down the chimney, his last name ought to be St. Nick.

"Kyle?" she called, her voice high-pitched. "I'll be waiting in the truck."

She heard him cross the room hurriedly. Suddenly he pulled the heavy mahogany door open—making the task look easier than it was for most people—and grinned at her. "I'm ready. I was just washing soot off my arms. I know you'll be thrilled when I finally get a change of clothes."

He shoved his arms into his grimy shirt. His chest and shoulder muscles flexed under a snug white thermal top that was smudged with sooty fingerprints across the flat plane of his stomach. The prints disappeared under the waistband of his jeans. They would have made an interesting roadmap for a trip through Surprise territory.

"Clean clothes. Yes," Sara said, distracted.

"What's in the basket?"

"A rabbit." Her palms were damper than the Amazon rain forest. Sara took a steadying breath. "I keep it in the lab."

He frowned quizzically as he buttoned his shirt with large, extraordinarily nimble fingers that must have had lots of experience in delicate maneuvers. Sara suspected that those fingers were adept at dismantling everything from locks and bombs to a woman's resistance.

"You don't perform some kind of animal experiments, do you?" he asked. "You're not injecting Bugs Bunny with carrot hormones, I hope."

Sara managed a laugh. "I'm not Dr. Frankenstein. No. The, uhmmm, rabbit is just a pet. Unfortunately, it keeps getting out of its cage. It likes rare tropical plants for lunch. So I'm giving it back to the original owner."

"I love rabbits." Kyle smiled fiendishly. "Broiled, with a side dressing of rice." Sara swept him with a look of mock dismay and took a step back. He chuckled. "Jep and I hunted rabbits when we were growing up." He paused for effect. "Beach bunnies."

Sara only smiled, afraid to laugh again because it might wake Noelle. "I can picture the Surprise brothers on the prowl together. The Great Blond Hunters, cruising the dangerous coast of Florida, armed with suntan lotion and a cooler full of beer."

"Not Jeopard. He was the only guy on the beach with a cooler of Dom Pérignon. *And* the only guy who needed absolutely nothing more than a smile to draw every female within sight."

Sara nodded, though she tried to picture Kyle's elegant, stern older brother lazing on the beach, carefree. She couldn't. Jeopard Surprise might have been fun-loving once, but the years had turned him into a tough, brooding enigma, frighteningly so. During the rescue attempt, before she'd realized that he was on her side, she'd lashed a well-aimed foot into his groin. He hadn't made a sound. He hadn't even looked upset. He had simply pushed her into the grip of a giant named Drake Lancaster, then leaned against a wall for a few seconds, his eyes nearly shut. The Iceman, she had heard Drake and Rucker call him.

"You love your brother very much, and you admire him," she said to Kyle. "I can hear that in your voice."

He nodded. "And I'm just as close to my sister Millie. The three of us pretty much raised each other. Our mother died when we were kids, and our old man put the navy first, the family second. But he was a hell of a guy." Kyle shrugged, any regrets resolved long ago.

"I think that you're the most interesting of the men in your family," Sara told him. "Probably the most creative too. So Jeopard used his perfect smile and expensive champagne to lure beach bunnies? What was your modus operandi?"

"I offered them milk," he assured her solemnly. "I went for the wholesome girls."

"Or maybe the girls with good teeth and big, uhmmm, bones."

He laughed richly. "Those too."

The beautiful masculine tones of his laughter made her giddy; they were like fine wine hitting her bloodstream. When he suddenly stepped into the hall, Sara moved quickly away from him, almost stumbling.

"I just want to look at your cottontail," he protested.

Sara put a hand over the spot where the picnic basket's lid had once, years before, had a clasp. "It's . . . it's wild. I can't open the basket."

"You keep a wild rabbit for a pet? Let me guess—it's a guard rabbit for the lab. All right, youse dirty thief"—he turned his voice into what could only, to Sara's rattled mind, be described as James Cagney doing Thumper—"drop the microscope or I'll mate with your wife's fuzzy bedroom slippers."

Sara covered her mouth to keep from either laughing or crying, she wasn't sure which. The strain of having Kyle so close to Noelle was beginning to tell.

"Your rabbit smells like you sprayed perfume on it," he commented, sniffing.

Baby powder. Sara winced inwardly. Damn this situation! Everything in her scientist's nature was devoted to finding and recognizing the truth. Weaving this ludicrous lie went against the principles of her orderly universe. And she was just plain lousy at it. She walked toward the great room, holding her picnic basket in front of her as if she could block the fragrance of scented talc.

"You smell Eau de Carrot," she said over her shoulder in a tone that meant drop the subject. "Hurry up. I'm leaving."

"Sara." He caught up with her, slipping into his dirty jacket as she entered a big foyer where the cold gray stone walls suited her mood. "Let me carry your killer bunny," he teased gently. "I didn't mean to upset you."

She shook her head but gave him a reassuring smile. "Just open the door and let the bridge down. The key's hanging on the horn over there."

From a short white horn mounted on a wall plaque he took a key ring so large that Sara could have put it over her head like a heavy necklace. It was made of wrought iron, with moons and stars worked into one quadrant of the circle. The ornate key contained the same design. The head of it filled the palm of Kyle's hand.

"When did you buy the place from the giant?" he asked dryly. Then he glanced at the horn. "Nice trophy. Caught a unicorn in the backyard, hmmm?"

"It came from an antelope." Sara felt Noelle shift inside the basket. "My brother and I found it on a family safari to Africa. I must have been about ten years old. The antelope had died from natural causes. But I do love unicorns. When I was very little my grandfather had me believing that they hid behind the trees in the garden. I knew that if I looked hard enough, I'd see them. I don't think I've ever given up hope. Open the door. This rabbit might get impatient."

The door's original bolt slid back with a ponderous creaking of iron on wood as Kyle turned the key. He studied the newer electronic lock next to the door handle. "Your code, m'lady."

"One four two, two two six."

He punched buttons. "Any mystical significance, sorceress?"

"Nope. It's just a combination of my IQ and birthday."

Kyle arched a brow at her. "You were born in January 1942?" Smiling wryly, she shook her head. He exhaled with relief. "February twenty-sixth?" She nodded. "So your IQ is only a modest genius level of one hundred and forty-two points?"

"Yes."

"Thank God. For a second I felt like a chimpanzee who's just found out he's been discussing bananas with Albert Einstein."

He pushed the door open. Sara pointed to a control panel on the wall of the outer foyer. "That operates the bridge."

She waited until she was certain that Kyle's attention was trained on the interesting spectacle of a hydraulic system lowering five yards of heavy wooden bridge across a moat filled with good old southern privet hedge. Then she lifted the basket lid and peeked inside. Noelle lay on her stomach sleeping soundly, just as before.

"What's up, Doc?"

Kyle's voice and footsteps startled her. She jumped and tried not to slap the lid down too loudly. Her nerves on fire, Sara frowned at him. "You . . . the rabbit . . . it . . . you could have made it jump out!"

He pointed to the alert dog near her feet. "Your crack security canine would have hunted it down." Daisy, who had fallen asleep during the two minutes it had taken them to unlock the door and lower the bridge, lay on her back, legs splayed.

Sara nudged her with the toe of a sneaker. "Wake up."

Daisy made a grunting sound and opened bleary eyes.

"Sounds like a security *pig* to me," Kyle noted cheerfully.

"Daisy!"

The dog got up, yawning, and trotted outside. Sara gazed at Kyle, feeling troubled. "You think that I and my useless guard dog are pretty ridiculous."

He shook his head, and the teasing glint faded from his eyes. "I think you're a gentle, loving person at heart, and you'd rather trust Daisy than bring any dragons into your home."

She nodded, a little shaken by his insight. He stepped aside and swept a hand toward the bridge. "After you, m'lady."

Sara had already brought the truck around from the back, where she kept it in a small shed. It waited on the cobblestone apron beyond the bridge. The tailgate and camper hatch were open. Noelle's car seat was hidden in the front corner of the truck bed, under a pile of blankets.

"Go ahead and get into the cab," she told Kyle. "I've got to tie this basket shut."

"Sure. We wouldn't want the killer bunny to get out."

The geese waddled around a corner of the castle. Sara stared at them in dismay. "Worry about the geese instead. Kyle, get in the truck!" As soon as they saw him, a stranger, they went into battle mode. They trotted forward, their wings spread, their heads thrust forward, their beady eyes never leaving their target.

He said a couple of words that were probably offensive to everything with wings, including airplanes. Then he snatched the picnic basket from Sara's hands and shoved it into the back of the truck. "I'll save you," he called, sounding a great deal more amused than she was at the moment. She expected to hear Noelle's wail of distress immediately.

He lifted Sara into the truck bed. Daisy leapt clumsily and landed in her lap. Kyle slammed the tailgate and ran to the driver's side of the cab. It was locked. He ran to the other side and tried the passenger door. It was locked.

He began to laugh. "I'm goose meat! I'm a goner!"

Sara scrambled out and unlocked the driver's door. She dove across the seat, reaching for the lock on the passenger door. Kyle slung it open and threw himself into her lap just as a big gander reached him, hissing and striking.

"He got me!" Kyle's head was pillowed on her thighs; he was laughing so hard that he couldn't sit up. His long legs dangled from the truck. In its beak the gander had trapped the laces on one of Kyle's running shoes. Sara grabbed a package of crackers from the glove compartment, ripped it open, and flung the contents out the passenger side. The gander let go of Kyle's laces and went after the treat.

Kyle swung the door shut and pushed himself up-right, then glanced down at her thighs as if he were remembering how they had felt under his head and deciding how they would feel under his hands. "Thank you, m'lady, thank you. You saved me from the drag-ons." He looked startled when she climbed out and headed toward the back.

"I'm just going to check on my rabbit." Her heart racing, Sara crawled into the truck bed and opened the picnic basket. Noelle chortled and smiled around her pacifier as Sara lifted her out and fastened her into the car seat. "Ride in here with Daisy for just a few min-utes, sweetheart," Sara whispered. "Then I'll come get you." She patted Daisy and wearily returned to the cab. "The rabbit is fine."

Kyle freed an object that had been wedged in the seat near his hip. "What's this?" he asked, holding it up. "A life preserver for a fairy?"

Sara stared at the pink teething ring in horror. The ring had disappeared last month, after their last shop-ping trip. Now she knew where Noelle had dropped it.

"It's a dog toy," she said weakly. She tossed the teething ring out the window.

Kyle chuckled dryly. "I didn't think that Daisy was smart enough to play with toys. She's a low form of plant life with fur. That's why you call her 'Daisy.' "

"She's just mellow. Very mellow." Sara cranked the truck hurriedly and drove down the cobblestone lane to the gate. She stopped, pulled a radio-control unit from her purse, and signaled a mechanism to roll the wide steel gate aside. Then she handed the unit to Kyle. "I have two. You keep this one as long as you're my guest."

"I feel like Walt Disney just gave me the key to the Magic Kingdom. Thanks, Tinker Bell."

After Sara drove through the gate he signaled it to close. As she put the truck in gear and started down the half-mile driveway to the road, she felt his gaze on her. "This remote control has your mother's initials written on it."

Sara nodded and said softly, "I'm sure she'd be proud to have you use it."

"Jep knew her a lot better than I did, since he was working on this end of the case. He was impressed with her."

"You mean he was impressed with her *after* he was certain that she wasn't working for . . . that she wasn't voluntarily involved in my herbicide research, that she was complying only for my sake."

"You really don't want to say his name. Are the memories so bad, Sara?"

"Yes." A very faint scratching noise made her glance toward the back. The window of the truck's cab looked directly into the front window of the camper. Only a few inches of space separated the two.

Daisy was clawing at the taped-down curtains on the camper window. When she parted the curtains and peered out happily, Sara stiffened with shock. She'd forgotten how much Daisy loved to watch the scenery. "Dai—" She caught herself. What if Kyle turned around to look? From his side he could see directly into the corner where she'd placed Noelle.

I know it's an odd-looking rabbit, Kyle. She has my nose and mouth, don't you think? And I really think she has my eyes, though they're dark brown, not green. They don't have any of her father's cruelty in them.

Sara could barely keep the truck centered in the driveway. She adjusted the rearview mirror so that she could stare into the camper window. Her mouth desert-dry, she watched Daisy disappear in Noelle's direction. Sara chewed her lip until it throbbed. *Oh, no, not now,* she begged. Daisy wasn't going to hurt Noelle, no, Daisy had an abiding love for Noelle's toys. She'd stolen more than a dozen of them already.

Daisy came back to the window. Clenched in her front teeth was Noelle's big yellow pacifier.

Kyle was saying, "So Brig McKay was put in the jail where Millie was working as a deputy. Here's this famous Australian country-western singer, used to having women fall at his feet, and my sister treats him like some kind of Saturday-night redneck. Brig told *People* magazine that he *had* to marry her—it was the only way he could get her to take his handcuffs off."

He told her about Millie and Brig's baby boy, and Sara nodded as if all her attention weren't riveted to the drama that was courting disaster for her baby girl. Daisy dropped the pacifier, picked it up again, and sat contentedly with it stuck in the front of her mouth.

She looked like somebody had put a stopper in her to keep stupidity from gushing out.

Sara gripped the steering wheel so hard that her hands hurt. Kyle hadn't paid much attention to the teething ring; he probably didn't even know what a teething ring was. But even a longtime bachelor could recognize a baby pacifier.

"Sara!" He grabbed the steering wheel. She realized that she'd narrowly missed hanging a front tire in the drainage ditch beside the driveway. A hundred yards ahead she could see the paved public road and the thick stone columns of the second gate.

"Sorry. I don't drive much anymore. I'm a little rusty."

Kyle held the wheel firmly, keeping the truck centered in the narrow drive. "Stop, Tinker Bell. Okay? Stop for a second. You're shaking all over."

She halted the truck. *Bluff,* she thought desperately, glancing in the back mirror. Daisy was now rolling the pacifier around in her mouth as if it were a big mint.

Kyle took her hand and caressed the back of it with his thumb. "It's not easy for you to leave the estate," he said gruffly. "I understand. Why don't you let me go with you today?"

Sara shut her eyes. Oh, God, he was so kind and caring, and she was leading him on with such lies! "No. It's really better that I go on alone. I have to prove that I can make it without help. Would you mind walking to your car from here?"

"No, if that would make you feel better." He sounded reluctant to let her go, but he was trying not to push her too hard, too fast. Sara tried to smile at him. His dark blue eyes were so sympathetic that it was all she could do to keep from tumbling heart first into the affection they offered.

"I'll be back in two or three hours," she promised.

"I'll be waiting. You've got my grocery list?"

She nodded, fighting an urge to look toward the camper window. Kyle gripped her hand tightly, his fingers slow and warm and just as nimble as she'd imagined, stroking the cup of her palm.

"See you later," Sara said desperately. "Come on. I'll walk a few yards with you."

Her knees were weak as she got out of the truck and shut the door. Kyle came around to her side. The scars accented his strong, expressive features in ways that made him look terribly forbidding when he frowned, as he was doing now.

"I don't think you can make this trip alone," he said, standing defiantly in front of her. He massaged the tops of her shoulders. "My God, you're tense. Sara, I'm sorry if I've sounded flippant about your problem before. I didn't realize how alone and how afraid you are. I'll help you get over it. I swear I'll help."

She grabbed his hand, led him a dozen steps beyond the front of the truck, put her arms around his neck and her head on his shoulder, then hugged him hard, standing on tiptoe as she forced every muscle to release its fear and absorb his comfort. He couldn't help her because he didn't know the truth. She'd never let him know, because she never wanted to look into those warm, sexy eyes and see contempt. But she wanted him to know how much his offer—no, how much *he* meant to her.

"You're the sweetest man I've ever known," she whispered. "And if I need help, I'll ask right away."

"So, uh, need a little help?" he murmured against her hair. He hugged her back, his arms taut bands of muscle around her, making her feel both safe and afraid.

"No, Sir Knight, not today." Sara patted his chest, and he understood the warning. Slowly he let her go. She stepped away, smiled at him, and exhaled wearily. "Watch out for the dragons."

"You too," he called as she staggered back to the truck. "You too."

Her shopping was blissfully uneventful. When she returned she found Kyle's sleek black sports car parked in front of the castle. Sara locked the back of the truck and left it filled with baby food and disposable diapers, all hidden inside plastic garbage bags. She'd unload them during the middle of the night.

The disposable diapers and plastic bags grated on her environmentalist's conscience, but she had to have them, just this once. With Kyle on hand she couldn't tote baby products around in open paper sacks. Nor could she wash loads of cloth diapers in the laundry room right off the kitchen.

Sara made certain that Noelle was fast asleep inside the wicker basket before she entered the castle, Daisy ambling along beside her. She strained her ears but heard no indication that Kyle was moving about. Maybe he was taking a nap. After all, he'd spent all night on the roof planning his invasion and chipping away at the mortar that held her chimney cap in place. Sighing with relief, Sara hurried to the nursery and settled

Noelle in her crib. Then she went back to the truck, got two small sacks filled with Kyle's grocery requests, and took them to the kitchen.

Afterward she cruised back toward the bedrooms. Outside his door she called, "Kyle?" in a polite tone, and knocked. When there was no answer she tested the doorknob. Unlocked. Sara glanced into the room. The end of his tote bag could be seen peeking from behind the heavy damask draperies on the sides of a kingly bedstead. His dirty clothes were draped over the shell of a knight who stood guard in one corner.

Sara's mouth twitched with amusement. The suit of armor was wearing Kyle's Hawaiian shirt.

But where was Kyle? As if in answer, Daisy woofed and trotted toward a tall, narrow window across the room. She put her front paws on its stone sill and reared up so that she could peer out the beveled glass. She woofed again.

Sara frowned and went to the window. And then she began to laugh. Earlier he had thought her geese so funny.

Across the garden Kyle sat astride the limb of a giant oak tree. He was looking down. Her attack geese were looking up.

Five

Stretched out on his stomach along the couch in front of her fireplace, Kyle shifted his legs slowly and winced. He felt Sara's hand pat his shoulder gently, and her sympathetic attention made his embarrassment even more acute. During the course of his old career he had outwitted some of the smartest terrorists in the world; now he couldn't outwit a flock of fat, waddling birds.

"What happened?" she asked.

He tried to sound grandly disgusted. "I came back, cleaned up, and decided to bring in some firewood."

"You should have taken my geese seriously after the way they chased you this morning."

"I thought they were all honk and no action."

Sara sat cross-legged in the floor, near enough that he could touch her if he wanted. He always wanted— even now, when the corners of her mouth kept curling upward at his expense.

"I only wanted to bring in some firewood. To be a good guest."

"I know. I promise not to laugh out loud anymore."

"I brought in two armloads from the woodpile without the geese noticing me. Then I got greedy. I went back for a third load. They noticed."

"And then?"

"They took revenge for every quill pen and down pillow ever made. They pinched me with those damned beaks. I haven't been grabbed so much since I rode to the top of the Empire State Building in an elevator full of drunk women."

"Would you like some liniment for your pained dignity?"

"Yes."

While she was out of the room he got up and gingerly padded to the huge hearth where he'd stacked his first two loads of firewood. The third lay scattered around the base of the tree he'd climbed.

By the time she came back, carrying a mysterious jar, he'd built a fire. The aromatic scent of burning oak filled the castle's great room. The room was suspended between pleasant shadows and the last of the afternoon sunlight that filtered through the tall windows on the southern side. Kyle leaned against the fireplace and thought how appealing the room was, especially when Sara stood near the windows, backlit with a halo of sunshine.

She had changed into a soft blue sweater and stretchy white ski pants with the instep straps turned up around her ankles. The outfit revealed a small, slender body curved with muscle. She was little but not fragile. Still, a man would want to be very gentle when he held her in bed.

Kyle's reverie dissolved as he pictured the imprints his ridged scars would leave on her skin. He'd never kiss her again; he wouldn't dredge up the subject of his ugliness. And he'd try not to daydream any more than he could help. But unbidden new images tormented him already. He and Sara, curled up together on the couch, sharing a mug of hot cider, her arms slipping around his neck, her mouth tasting of apple and cinnamon . . .

"Lie down again," she ordered him, her expression fathomless. "And tell the nice sorceress where the trolls nibbled at you."

"I can manage alone." Feeling troubled when he realized that she meant to rub the liniment on him, he decided that belligerence was a good defense.

She rolled her eyes. "After you came down from the tree you mentioned that your lower back hurt. You can't rub liniment on your own back."

"Maybe I have double-jointed arms."

"Maybe you have a thick head. Pull your shirt off. Lie down. Quit grumbling."

He eyed the jar she held. It was full of a slimy white substance. "You're going to turn me into a garden slug. When I walk I'll leave a trail. What is that stuff?"

"It's the juice of a plant that grows in the Amazon rain forest. It's been used for centuries by the Indians there. It won't hurt you."

"My sister Millie said that to me once, when we were kids. A Surprise never turns down a chance to take chances. We taste-tested some swamp water. I don't want to go into the ugly details, but the people who sell milk of magnesia made a lot of money as a result of that experiment."

She looked at him patiently but tapped a bare, dainty foot on the scroll pattern of a richly ornamented rug. "I haven't got all afternoon, Kyle."

Before the incident in Surador he had never been self-conscious about his body. He had kept himself in good shape, admired the results in a full-length mirror occasionally, but otherwise never thought about it except when someone, invariably female, offered a compliment. Confidence, not vanity, had made him feel comfortable.

Now he had to grit his teeth to keep from hesitating any longer. Kyle jerked a ribbed white sweater over his head and lay down on the old couch, feeling its cool, soft leather meet his scarred chest and stomach. He wished that the loose brown corduroys he wore didn't hang so low on his waist.

He pillowed his head on one forearm and stared resolutely at his own bicep, trying not to think about the fact that Sara had just knelt on the thick tapestry rug beside the couch, that she must be grimacing at what Diego de Valdivia's well-trained dogs had accomplished.

"I . . . I think you're right," she said abruptly. "I think you can put the liniment on without my help." She set the jar on the floor and vaulted to her feet as Kyle raised his head to stare at her. "I'll be in my lab until six. Your chili fixings are waiting for you in the kitchen."

She turned and left the room quickly, without looking back. Kyle's hands knotted into fists as humiliation and sorrow poured through him. *Now try to tell me that you don't mind my scars, Sara.*

Noelle mouthed a spoonful of crushed ice and frowned. Tears still gleamed in her dark eyes, and her face looked ready to crumple again at any second. Sara rocked her in a big chair next to the nursery window. Exhausted from the day's traumas, Sara meditated on the sunset and nearly dozed off.

"Mice," Noelle told her.

Ice. Sara dipped the spoon into a cup on the windowsill. Noelle took it eagerly and held her mouth open as Sara rubbed a bit over the tiny nubs of two front teeth. In all of medical science there ought to be something to treat sore teeth.

For two hours Noelle had alternately eaten ice and cried. Lying on the sill was the tiny, flesh-colored transmitter Sara had been wearing in one ear when the teething crisis began. Her ear still rang from Noelle's high-pitched wails.

Poor Kyle, he must have been disgusted at her for changing her mind about the rubdown. But there had been no way she could ignore Noelle's angry shrieks, especially not when the transmitter had magnified and then focused them on one lone eardrum. She had almost run from the room because she feared that the transmitter was so loud Kyle could hear Noelle too.

Noelle nestled her head against Sara's chest and sighed as Sara's fingers stroked her hair soothingly. Too tired to fight sore gums any longer, her eyes drooped shut. She was asleep by the time Sara put her in the crib and kissed her softly on one cheek.

Sara looked at her watch. Almost six o'clock. Good timing. She could eat dinner with Kyle and make certain that he hadn't read anything odd into her actions. She couldn't judge their effect herself; her senses were numb from the day's events. She did know one thing—despite the risk and inconvenience of having him as a guest, she felt a tingle of anticipation that made new energy hum through her veins now.

Sara tucked the transmitter back into her ear, pulled several wisps of hair over it, and checked the listening unit that hung on the wall beside Noelle's crib. Thank goodness for technology. Unlike people, it behaved in predictable ways.

The kitchen was full of cheerful light and delicious smells. Kyle sat at the table by the bay window, his feet propped on the window seat and his hands latched behind his head. After Sara padded silently into the room she realized that he was either watching the sunset intently or was so lost in thought he hadn't heard her approach.

A pair of leather hiking boots lay upended on the floor, and his feet were covered only in white crew socks. He presented a relaxed, unforbidding image, but hardly a tame one. His torso looked trim but powerful in the handsome white sweater, his long legs provoked her interest even encased in loose brown trousers, and his tousled hair was a sensual lure for her fingers. "Hello," he said without turning around.

Sara jumped. "How did you know I was here?"

He pulled his feet down and swiveled in his chair. "We highly trained James-Bond types pick up on the tiniest nuance of sound." He added dryly, "And I saw your reflection in the window."

She was puzzled by the expression in his eyes. Even though he sounded cheerful he looked sad, or maybe resigned. She couldn't tell for certain. Her gaze moved to a pair of empty beer bottles on the table. Obviously he was in the mood for something stronger than his whimsical chocolate sodas.

Sara fumbled for neutral conversation. "I did get the right brand of beer, didn't I? And the Coco-Moos? That was right?"

"Sure. Thanks."

She went to the stove and lifted the lid on a large pot. "Oh, Kyle. Oh. Hmmmm. You outdid yourself. To a person who would starve if it weren't for frozen food and microwave ovens, homemade chili is heaven."

"Well, Jeopard couldn't cook and Millie wasn't very good at it either. I was the designated chef when we were growing up. Do you want to eat at the table with me, or are you going back to the lab?"

"I have time to eat with you."

"Look, it's okay if you don't. I understand. I've been here only one day. I know it's going to take a while for you to, well, to adjust to me."

She chuckled. "You make yourself sound like a strange new pet."

"A different sort of dragon, maybe."

"You're no dragon," she corrected him, frowning at his choice of descriptions. She nodded toward the stove and smiled awkwardly. "I smell enough chili powder to make me think we'll both be able to breath fire soon."

"My chili is good for what ails you. I think it kills germs. Or maybe it just scares the hell out of them."

"Speaking of ailments, how are your goose bites?"

"Fine. That liniment did help."

"Did you get enough of it on your back? I'll be glad to—"

"It's fine," he said quickly.

"I'm sorry I ran out on you. I'd forgotten about an experiment I needed to check."

"No explanation needed." He rose, looking restless. There were times, such as now, when Sara glimpsed the intensity that he hid under his casual facade. This was, after all, a man who had lived dangerously for most of his adult life. She feared that he was already bored by his Good Samaritan role and its confinement.

"There's a portable television set in one of the bedrooms," she told him. "The reception inside these walls isn't too great, but there's a VCR, too, and I have a big collection of tapes—mostly classics and PBS specials—but you're welcome to watch them if you want."

He looked at her ruefully and put his hands on his hips. "What? No Popeye cartoons or reruns of *Gilligan's Island* for us ordinary folks to enjoy?"

"I wasn't trying to imply that you wouldn't appreciate highbrow entertainment. Why are you so defensive tonight?"

He shook his head, and his shoulders slumped a little. He looked apologetic. "I'm just moody these days. Remember, I'm here to rehabilitate my own attitude as well as yours."

Sara crossed her arms over her chest with mock command. "Tell me what's wrong with your attitude."

He eyed her warily. "I make chili as a way of expressing myself. Understand my chili, and you'll understand me."

"You won't be a mystery for very long, then. Let's eat."

She set the kitchen table with heavy crockery bowls and pewter serving pieces engraved with the Scarborough family crest. Kyle got another beer; she opened her first, in fact the first one she'd had since before her pregnancy. Being the sole caretaker of a baby, a castle, and a research lab was a constant responsibility; she was afraid to mellow out, even a little. She always had too much to do.

But tonight was special. Kyle ladled chili into their bowls and carried the pot back to the stove. After he sat down he raised his beer and said, "A toast. I'll make one, then you make one."

"Okay." She held her bottle up.

He clinked his to it. "To better times for us both."

Tears stung the corners of Sara's eyes. "To good memories rather than bad."

"To the future of plastic surgery."

Sara eyed him gently. She tapped her bottle to his with a little too much force. "To the happiness that exists in the present."

He glared at the way she brandished her beer bottle. "What is this, a challenge? The duel of the Budweisers?"

Chuckling, Sara put her beer down and ate a spoonful of chili. She glanced up and caught Kyle watching her closely. "Well, what do you think?" he demanded.

"About your attitude, as expressed in your chili? Hmmm. Pretty hot, but so well-balanced that it doesn't burn. Patiently prepared. Contains a few unexpected ingredients that make it more complicated than it seems on the surface. All in all, I'm quite impressed."

He looked pleased. "But the important question is, does it make you hungry for more?"

Hungry? She was starving, but not for chili. "Oh, ho. A leading question. It strains the comparison too far."

"Evasive woman," he grumbled. "If *your* attitude was a meal, what would it be?"

She grinned. "Oysters. Still in the shell."

"I'm an expert at opening oysters."

"Are you an oyster connoisseur, or just a pearl thief?"

"Both."

This was like an Italian trapeze act, Sara thought. The Flying Innuendos. It was dangerous for the untrained to attempt, and her recklessness was going to send her for a hard fall. "Eat your attitude before it gets cold," she ordered.

And then, like a woman enjoying a wonderful meal after a long, dull diet, she put a large spoonful of chili into her mouth and smiled with guilty pleasure.

Since his cooking provoked such an interesting exchange of information, Kyle got up before dawn the next morning to fix breakfast. She'd mentioned that she was an early bird, as he was, but he couldn't imagine that she'd be out classifying species of worms *this* early. He drew a pair of jeans and a white sweatshirt over his thermal underwear, put on two pairs of socks, and padded out of his room, shivering a little. Central heating didn't do a hell of a lot of good in a castle.

He was startled to see the kitchen light on; even more startled to find her asleep with her head on the kitchen table, a half-finished cup of coffee sitting near one outflung hand. A blue robe covered her from neck to ankles. Kyle pressed his lips together tightly to keep from laughing when he saw her sophisticated footwear.

Dr. Scarborough favored giant, fuzzy, tiger-striped bedroom slippers with whiskers and plastic eyes on the fronts. Those shoes endeared her to him. He would have loved to stroke her hair, but that being too much like a caress, he simply shook her shoulder a little. "Wake up, tiger-toes."

"Morning," she said raspily, squinting up at him.

He frowned at the exhaustion in her face. "Did you work all night?"

She nodded, looking dazed and groggy. "Most."

"Why?"

"Uhmmm, uhmmm . . ." She frowned, moved her hands around on the table in vague patterns as if sorting through answers, and finally said, "My plants are like babies. Uh-huh. You never know when they're going to grow teeth." Satisfied with that explanation, she put her head down on the table and fell asleep again.

"Plants with teeth," Kyle teased under his breath. "I hope there's a rabies shot for philodendrons." He took her under both arms and lifted her to her feet.

Her chin and eyelids rose slowly, until she could finally see him. "Hmmm?"

"I'm going to carry you to your bedroom."

"Good plan."

He scooped both arms under her and lifted her easily. With her softness cradled against him and her head resting trustingly on his shoulder he could have carried her to the next state and back if she'd wanted him to. He caught the scent of her unusual perfume again; he'd never smelled anything quite like it before. It reminded him of the sweet, milky smell of a puppy—which was a compliment, though he doubted she'd agree. Few women wanted to be told that they smelled like a dog.

He walked through the great room and entered the main hallway. When he reached the double doors of her suite he tested them with a foot, and one swung open. From the corner of his eye he noted that the strange extra door in one wall was shut . . . and undoubtedly locked.

But mysterious doors were the least of his concerns at the moment. He carried Sara to the bed, a queen-size model atop a simple base of dark wood. It was neatly covered in a green comforter with delicate print sheets that peeked out at the top. There was very little evidence that she'd slept on it the night before.

She sank gratefully onto the comforter and burrowed her head on a pillow encased in material that matched the sheets. Everything about her and her bed was fresh and neat and wholesome, Kyle thought, but it wasn't a prim, don't-touch wholesomeness.

On the contrary, with the incandescent light of dawn slipping over her she looked infinitely touchable. He made a low sound of frustration as his body tightened into a fierce protest against *not* touching her. Kyle busied himself by pulling the comforter and sheets out from under her.

She murmured a compelling sound of appreciation when he removed her funny slippers. He couldn't let the harmless opportunity pass, so he rubbed her feet.

"Oh, Kyle." She sighed, sounding as if he'd just brought her to a peak of pleasure.

All right, so she knew what was happening and she wasn't unhappy about it. That didn't mean she wanted anything more. His hands trembling with restraint, he draped the bed coverings across her legs. He halted, staring at the thick terry-cloth tie around the waist of her robe. He ought to quit torturing himself right now and leave the room.

But he told himself he was in control; there wasn't anything wrong with just loosening her robe to make her more comfortable. Besides, he could see the neck of a floppy gray sweatshirt between the lapels. She certainly wouldn't be embarrassed to have him see more of *that*.

"Do you want me to help you take your robe off?" he whispered, trying to sound unaffected by the desperate heat racing through his body.

Her eyes still shut, she frowned as if thinking, but the limp-wristed way she dragged a hand over her forehead showed that nothing was coordinating very well. "Sure," she said eventually, and tried to help by fumbling with her tie.

He gently pushed her hands away and unfastened the knot. Unappealing sweatshirt regardless, his breath caught as he eased the robe apart. Her breasts were pert, pointed mounds under the soft material, and the area between the bottom of her shirt and the top of the bedcovers revealed several inches of sleek thigh and a hint of black silk panties.

Come-hither lingerie, a sweatshirt, and goofy-looking slippers with whiskers. The woman was sexy, athletic, and disarmingly unconcerned about having silly feet. It was a great combination. "Sit up, Sara," he ordered softly. "Pull your arms out of the robe."

She managed to prop herself up until he got the robe off. Then she sank back, tugged the covers up to her waist, and made an *mmmm* sound of happiness. Kyle tried to set a world record for procrastination as he fiddled with the robe, straightening it, folding it, unfolding it, and finally arranging it on the far corner of the bed, just so. He hated to leave her. Without touching her, without hoping for anything, he'd just like to stand and watch her sleep.

But he knew that he'd look ludicrous—worse, lecherous—if she woke up enough to realize that he was staring at her like a man who'd never seen a woman before. Plus waking up to his face wouldn't exactly make her day.

"Sweet dreams," he said, bending over her. He very lightly tucked the covers around her waist.

"Kyle." She sounded more as if she were dreaming than awake. Her hand settled on top of his, and the fingers stroked languidly, moving over a small white scar without hesitation.

His breath stalled when she pulled his hand to her lips and kissed the palm, her lips soft and incredibly smooth. The blood pounded in his ears. It wasn't just his loneliness or the basic need for a woman's touch that destroyed his control; it was Sara, sweet, strong

Sara, who posed so many mysteries but offered so many answers.

Kyle cupped her face in his hand, turned it toward him, and held her gently while he lowered his mouth onto hers. He gave her a slow, thorough kiss that explored every fraction of her lips; a constantly changing kiss that tugged and caressed, slipping back and forth over her mouth, finding she was instantly agreeable. Her tender and giving response blinded him with feelings that he'd never had before, an intense blending of desire and emotion that brought tears to his eyes.

He sat down beside her, still kissing her and being kissed back, now with growing wildness as she became more awake. Her arms circled his neck and began to pull him closer. Renewed confidence sent happiness scorching through him. She needed him. They needed each other, and together they could erase every memory of Diego de Valdivia.

Kyle put one arm under her shoulders and rested a hand on her shirt, then sought one of her breasts and rubbed it with a very light, tantalizing pressure. She moaned against his mouth and arched her back; Kyle smiled, feeling giddy with amazement over her reaction. He lifted her a little and began to ease the sweatshirt up.

Abruptly her eyes opened, wide, startled, and directly on his ravaged features. One hand slid to the side of her head; she tugged at the wisps of hair over one ear as if she had to make sure it was she who was really on the verge of making love with him.

"No," she said, her voice and eyes anguished, but firm.

Kyle froze inside as the true scenario became evident. She hadn't thought too much about what was happening until she woke up enough to remember what he looked like. Until now she'd simply been indulging her own desperate need for pleasure and affection. Now she saw; now she remembered; now she couldn't go any further.

"I would never do anything to hurt you," she whispered hoarsely. "You'd better go back to your own room." She still held her hand against one side of her head, as if she wanted to shake it in disbelief but wouldn't give in to the urge.

"You're killing me with kindness, Sara," he answered with a low, harsh chuckle. "But I appreciate the honesty. I think."

"If things were different in my life . . ." She let her voice trail off.

Kyle searched her eyes. *You mean if I weren't so hard to look at.* He knew he had to be philosophical. Bitterness was no good and would only lead to self-pity, if it hadn't already. He wasn't sure what he felt right now, but he resolved never, never to embarrass either himself or Sara with another display like this.

"I'm sorry," he told her. "It won't happen again." That was one of the oldest lines in the world, but he meant it.

"I'm so sorry," she answered, and tears slid from the corners of her eyes. She shook her head, still holding her hand flat over one side of it. "So sorry. You can't know how much."

Kyle eased himself away from her and stood up. "Believe me, I know," he said. He heard her crying as he left the room.

Six

The incident taught her a new lesson about Kyle, one that made her watch him with adoring eyes. As the days passed, he never mentioned the heated moment again; he never even hinted at it. This man didn't brood, nor did he put up angry defenses to torment her.

Even though she had hurt him, rejected him, and undoubtedly bewildered him, he was still determined to rescue her from her seclusion. He was still her friend, and she could depend on him for help of any kind, anytime.

She couldn't accept that help. She couldn't encourage him to stay. If she treated him cruelly, it was for his own good. And Noelle's.

So Sara stayed away, avoiding every opportunity to talk to him, refusing to let him draw her out of her lab except for an occasional meal. She spent all her waking hours exploring worlds she could control, or at least view objectively. Struggling to put order back into her thoughts, she drove herself relentlessly. The slides under her microscope brought forth answers even when nothing in her confused emotions made sense. Research was soothing, distracting. If only she were as good at examining and cataloging her feelings.

"You've made me a desperate man," Kyle announced one night toward the end of his first week at the castle. They had just finished dinner. She was headed back to her lab.

He stepped in front of the door that led from the great room. Blocking her exit without the least bit of hesitation, he crossed his arms over his chest in a gesture of resistance. He wore a red plaid shirt, jeans, leather suspenders, and his hiking boots. Sara thought he looked like an angry lumberjack eyeing a tree that refused to fall.

"How can I help you if I never see you?" he asked.

Sara sidled over to the fireplace, watching him cautiously. She felt small and trapped. His blue eyes gleamed with fierce determination.

"You just saw me," she said lightly. "We just ate dinner together. Vegetable soup and corn bread, remember? And we talked about music. You refused to believe that plants *love* Barry Manilow."

"I want to talk about *you*. That's what I came to Kentucky to do."

"Me? All right. I like Barry Manilow, but if I want my branches to grow faster, I listen to Bon Jovi."

Sara tugged at the neck of her pink sweater. Inside it her skin felt too warm, as it often did when she was with Kyle. She tried to look calm.

"Have a seat," he ordered, nodding toward the couch.

"And if I don't want to?"

"Then you can stand up while we talk." He pointed to the thick wooden beams overhead. "You can hang from the ceiling. Or crawl under a chair. Whatever. But you *will* talk to me."

Sara sank into one corner of the couch. He sat down on the big hearth rug, between her and the fire. Her eyes filled with tears of admiration at the way firelight shot gold and copper streaks through his hair. The shadows obscured his scars; she suspected that he had chosen that spot because of the shadows.

"I warned you that I wouldn't have much time to visit," Sara reminded him. "You knew that from the first."

"You're deliberately avoiding me, just like you've avoided the rest of the world for the past nineteen months."

"No, I—"

"Tell me something. Did you go to your mother's funeral?"

Sara flinched. "No, I didn't."

"My God." He was silent, frowning as he studied her. "Don't you see how much you need help? You let strangers bury her because you were afraid to leave this place."

Old misery welled up, fresh and painful inside her chest. He'd never know the agonies she had gone through while her mother's body lay in a New York morgue. Her only consolation had been the secure belief that her mother understood, that her mother knew that Sara had no one with whom to leave Noelle and no way to hide her from the curious attendees at a funeral.

"Mother didn't attach much importance to ceremonies," Sara said dully. Kyle must think she was heartless, she realized. "When my father and brother were killed in the Arctic storm, she and I went into the garden here and planted two oak trees. Among the roots of one my mother put my father's favorite pipe; under the second tree she put my brother's high school baseball cap. That was our memorial service, and it was perfect."

"You were too afraid of the outside world to go to your mother's funeral," Kyle insisted, emphasizing each word between clenched teeth.

"There was no need for me to go. Her body was

cremated. That's how she wanted it. One of her dearest friends—an old colleague from her university days—took the ashes to a park and spread them among the flowers."

"That should have been your duty, don't you think?"

Yes, Sara screamed silently. *But keeping Anna's granddaughter a secret from government investigators was my duty too.*

"I simply had no need to express my grief in a morbid ceremony. Sometimes I think you don't understand me very well, Kyle. Maybe you ought to realize that I'm happy being alone. And that I'm not a very sentimental person."

He described that claim with one blunt word. Sara gazed at him unhappily. Was there any way to bridge the gap between her desperate need for his affection and her equally desperate need to keep him from knowing about Noelle?

She jumped as the transmitter in her left ear produced an ominous succession of sounds from the nursery—Daisy barking, Noelle making gleeful noises, a loud crack as something hit the floor, and then static as the transmitter went dead.

Sara stood up. *Act calm. Be nonchalant.* "Good night."

"What the hell?" He vaulted to his feet. His long, easy strides beat her to the hallway door. He flung an arm across the opening so quickly that she ran into it.

Sara gazed up at him worriedly. "I have to go. Thanks for dinner. It was great."

"You're not going anywhere, Tinker Bell. Tonight you're sitting and talking. No argument."

"Kyle, I can't! I have an experiment—"

"Forget it. I don't believe you. You probably go back there and sit in front of your damned television sets and spy on me with cameras you've got hidden in the house."

"I'm not *that* eccentric! And if there were cameras

inside the house, I'm sure you would have found them by now. You'd have done another striptease and then cut the cables!"

He thrust his jaw forward belligerently. His mouth thinned with impatience. "Just what have you got in your lab? Hmmm? Go ahead and check on it. I'll go with you."

"Please, please." She sank her hands into the front of his shirt. "You promised that you wouldn't intrude on that part of my life. You *swore* that you wouldn't." She touched a finger to a scar on his cheek. "You swore on these, remember?"

He twisted his face away from her touch, but looked at her with grim acknowledgment. "All right," he said wearily. Then his fingers snaked forward and plucked the tiny transmitter from her ear.

"No! Give that back!"

"I noticed this a day or two ago, but I tried not to indulge my curiosity. What are the plants saying tonight, Sara?"

She tried to grab the device. He held it beyond her reach and braced a restraining hand against her shoulder. Frustration and concern for Noelle's predicament brought a string of harsh words from Sara's mouth.

"Very creative, Doctor," Kyle said pleasantly. "I've never been called names by a genius before. I'm honored." He put the transmitter into his ear and listened for a second. "The begonias are tampering with the radio again. It's not tuned to a station."

"Please let me go," she begged, bowing her head to his shoulder, all dignity lost. "I'll do anything you want, later. Right now just please give me that transmitter and let me go to the . . . to my lab."

Sara stared up into his face and knew that Jeopard wasn't the only one in the Surprise family who could look as inscrutable as a sphinx. Then a flicker of victory shown in Kyle's eyes, and he smiled thinly. "You'll eat every one of your meals with me from now on," he told her.

"All right."

"You'll give me at least two hours after dinner every night, just so that we can sit and talk."

"Fine."

"And tomorrow we'll drive over to Lexington and spend the whole afternoon. I bet you haven't been to a decent-size city in months."

That trip would be impossible. But Sara nodded numbly because all she cared about at the moment was getting to the nursery. "It's a deal."

He placed the transmitter in her hand. His fingers closed snugly around hers. "Scout's honor?"

"Yes."

He grunted. "You were never a scout. There aren't any troops for ten-year-olds who work calculus problems for fun. And no merit badges in advanced botany."

"You have my word," she said, wincing because she knew she would have to break it.

"Good enough." He let go of her hand and stepped back. "Go to the lab. I'll see you at seven for breakfast."

When she reached the nursery she sagged with relief. Noelle was standing up in her crib, holding the bars and bobbing in place merrily. Her yellow sleepsuit made her look like an excited Easter chick.

Daisy sat on the floor beside the fallen monitoring unit, a small device that resembled a walkie-talkie. Daisy's ears drooped, as if she feared that Sara might accuse her of knocking it off the wall.

Sara picked up a brightly colored rubber frog that lay suspiciously near the monitor. It was one of Noelle's crib toys. "I think that this frog has learned how to fly," Sara said dryly. Noelle squealed and gave her a dimpled smile. "I think that this frog flew over and kissed the baby monitor."

She put the toy aside to be washed. The monitor was

unharmed; the nursery's thick white carpet had cushioned its fall. She hung it back on the wall and made a mental note to fasten it tighter.

Now that the crisis was over she felt drained of energy, and a different kind of anxiety grew in her chest. "Let's watch the moon," Sara said wearily. She turned the nursery lights off and carried Noelle to the window.

A huge white moon cast its magical light on the shrubs and trees around the keep; it carved weird, sharp shadows on the wall beyond. The ethereal white guardian, riding high above the mountains, had inspired her grandfather Scarborough to name the place Moonspell Keep.

The moon and the setting had enchanted him, he said. Enchantment wasn't a bad thing, he thought. A world surrounded by magic was bound to a safe place. Gazing up into the eerie silver glow, Sara could easily believe that. Perhaps the moon would enchant Kyle and soften his misguided determination to help her.

Kyle waited for her patiently the next morning, sitting in the kitchen with a pot of coffee and a bowl of pancake batter ready. Seven o'clock came and went. At ten after Kyle strode to her bedroom door and knocked. There was no answer and no sound of movement behind the door. He went back to the kitchen and put the pancake batter in the refrigerator.

At twenty after he unplugged the coffeepot. Smiling thinly, so disgusted that he didn't care about the consequences of his actions, he went to her bedroom door and picked the lock, using a highly sophisticated tool he'd mastered over the years—a fingernail file.

The room was empty, though the unmade bed showed that she had at least spent the night there. The mysterious door to her secret part of the castle was shut and locked, just as he'd assumed it would be. Kyle inspected the electronic lock with its panel of numbered buttons. Hmmm. Since he didn't have the code, he'd need something a little more sophisticated than a fingernail file.

He froze at the sound of footsteps in the hallway behind the door and decided to give her one more chance. He trotted from the bedroom, locked the outer door again, and returned to the kitchen.

Five minutes later she hurried in, greeting him with a big smile as she tucked a blue cotton shirt into snug jeans. "I'm sorry!" She fluffed her short red hair as if she hadn't had time to comb it. "I overslept!"

"No, you didn't," he said cheerfully, going to plug the coffeepot in again. "You were in the back taking care of whatever it is you take care of so secretively."

Her hands froze around her face. "How . . . what makes you say that?"

"Intuition." He got out the bowl of pancake batter and put a griddle on the stove top. "Don't be late again."

"Don't get carried away with this takeover of yours! Are you going to time me?"

Smiling, he turned around and waved a spatula at her. "If you're more than five minutes late, I'll do my best to break into your lab and see what's keeping you."

He was immediately sorry that he'd made that threat. Her green eyes filled with anger, but also with fear. She looked horrified and worried. Kyle felt sorry for her.

She muffled a cry of distress behind one hand and went to the window seat, where she curled her legs under her and hugged both arms around her midsection. She seemed very lost and alone as she stared out at a bleak, overcast day.

"Sara," Kyle said in a soothing tone. He went over and sat down beside her, then stroked her shoulders with one hand. "I'm not an enemy. I'll keep your secrets—whatever they are. What are you so afraid of?"

"So many people have suffered because of me," she

whispered brokenly, her throat flexing. She continued to stare rigidly out the window, but tears slid down her cheeks. "Dinah was kidnapped because she happened to be my friend; my mother's health was ruined because she spent a year worrying about my safety; and you"—she struggled for control—"you were hurt badly because of me." She shook her head fiercely. "I don't want anyone else to suffer because of what I did."

"You were innocent."

"No. I was foolish. I took too many risks. Now I'm afraid that if anything ever happens again—to me—that more people will get hurt. I can't bear that idea."

"What people?"

"Anyone who's close to me."

Kyle slowly placed his hand on the back of her neck. He caressed with small circular motions and hoped that she wouldn't worry that the gesture was offering something besides comfort. "You can't go through the rest of your life alone, Tinker Bell."

"Maybe not. But I can try."

"Don't you ever want a family? A husband, kids?"

"Children?" She avoided the husband issue but looked at Kyle with an intensity he hadn't expected. "For years I didn't know if I wanted to be a mother. I couldn't decide if I'd be any good at it." She hesitated, seeming reluctant to say more. "What do you think about having kids?"

"I think I've missed my chance."

"You're a young man!"

Kyle had never considered himself much of a family type. Maybe the fierce longing that grew inside his chest now was provoked by Jeopard's upcoming marriage. Maybe it was provoked by wanting Sara more than he'd ever wanted anyone in his life. He thought of the terrified little boy in the country store. Maybe he should go take a look in the mirror and jerk himself back to reality.

"I don't do very well with kids," he muttered.

She gasped softly, and when he studied her eyes he saw that she understood his meaning. Kyle managed to shrug as if it were something he could easily accept. "I've gotten used to it. My sister's little boy cries every time he sees me. It's uncomfortable for him, and me too."

"How old is he?"

"He just had his first birthday."

"Oh, Kyle, at that age children are likely to be shy with strangers. They're starting to form distinct likes and dislikes, and sometimes they're so erratic that you can't *ever* figure them out. Don't let your nephew's reaction worry you."

Suddenly she took his face between her hands. Kyle stiffened with self-defense. He wouldn't let himself feel anything, even though she was gazing at him so tenderly that he wanted to kiss her.

"You'll marry some very lucky woman someday, and you'll have children," she assured him. "And they'll adore you."

He pulled her hands down. "I won't invade your lab if you won't touch my face."

"Kyle, you don't think that your scars have anything to do with my reasons—"

"I don't want to talk about it." He forced a smile and squeezed out of her hands. "So, Doc. You seem know a lot about babies. Let me guess—you're bottle-feeding a litter of geraniums in the lab. Tell me where you learned so much about motherhood."

Her skin was fair; it revealed changes in her mood with a speed that amazed him. Right now it was like watching color radar on a weather map. A cold front had just arrived.

"What's for breakfast?" she asked sharply. "Pancakes and interrogation? Is it going to be like this at every meal?"

"Not if you come to the table on time." Puzzled by her sharp reaction to an innocent question, he got up and went to the stove. "Lunch is at twelve. We'll drive over to Lexington after that. I'm tired of having dishpan hands, so I'll take you out to dinner."

"There's something I forgot to tell you last night. My groceries are being delivered this afternoon. Remember Tom and Lucy Wayne, the couple I've mentioned? They'll bring the supplies. Then Lucy will do some housework, and Tom's going to rake leaves."

"So you're saying that you want to postpone the trip?"

Kyle eyed her warily when she came over to him and leaned against the counter, smiling sweetly. "Could we go to Lexington tomorrow?" she asked, her elf's face looking too sincere. "Just think. I won't be in the lab this afternoon. I'll be right here, with you and Tom and Lucy. When they're not looking, you can twist my arm and try to make me answer more questions. You'll get to pester me all afternoon."

He pursed his lips. "Okay. That sounds like fun."

"I thought you'd like the idea."

She poured a cup of coffee and walked to the table. Her jeans contained an unmistakable and very sassy sway of victory. He decided to let her enjoy it while she could.

Tom and Lucy Wayne were simple, gentle people who worked hard and asked few questions. Their presence at the keep provided a welcome emotional buffer. Kyle, silent and brooding, went outside and helped Tom rake leaves. Sara dusted windows but found herself peering out distractedly, watching Kyle work.

"I'm r-ready for th-the wax, S-Sara."

Lucy Wayne's timid voice startled her. Sara smiled at her reassuringly. "Sorry. I forgot. It's right there." Sara pointed to a plastic bottle on the dining room table.

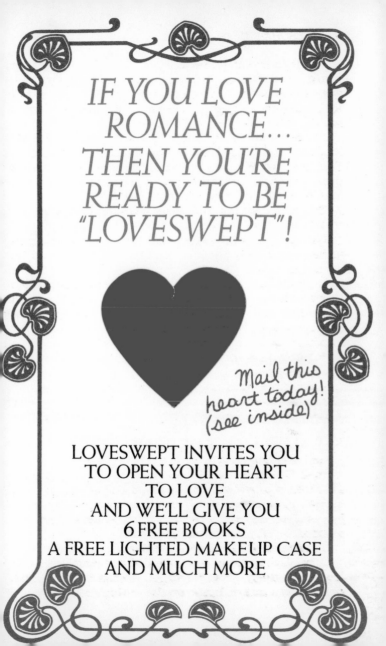

OPEN YOUR HEART TO LOVE...
YOU'LL BE LOVESWEPT
WITH THIS FREE OFFER!

HERE'S WHAT YOU GET:

1. **FREE!** SIX NEW LOVESWEPT
NOVELS! You get 6 beautiful stories filled with
passion, romance, laughter, and tears... exciting
romances to stir the excitement of falling in love...
again and again.

2. **FREE!** A BEAUTIFUL MAKEUP CASE
WITH A MIRROR THAT LIGHTS UP!
What could be more useful than
a makeup case with a mirror that
lights up*? Once you open the
tortoise-shell finish case, you have
a choice of brushes... for your lips,
your eyes, and your blushing
cheeks.
*(batteries not included)

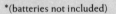

3. **SAVE!** MONEY-SAVING HOME
DELIVERY! Join the Loveswept at-home reader
service and we'll send you 6 new novels each month.
You always get 15 days to preview them before you
decide. Each book is yours for only $2.09 — a savings of
41¢ per book.

4. BEAT THE CROWDS! You'll always receive
your Loveswept books before they are available in
bookstores. You'll be the first to thrill to these exciting
new stories.

**BE LOVESWEPT TODAY — JUST COMPLETE,
DETACH AND MAIL YOUR FREE-OFFER CARD.**

FREE – LIGHTED MAKEUP CASE!
FREE – 6 LOVESWEPT NOVELS!

- NO OBLIGATION
- NO PURCHASE NECESSARY

(DETACH AND MAIL CARD TODAY.)

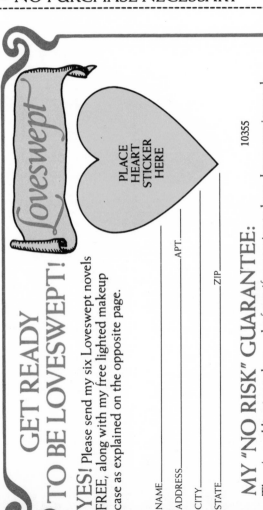

GET READY
TO BE LOVESWEPT!

YES! Please send my six Loveswept novels FREE, along with my free lighted makeup case as explained on the opposite page.

NAME _____

ADDRESS _____ APT. _____

CITY _____

STATE _____ ZIP _____

10355

MY "NO RISK" GUARANTEE:

There's no obligation to buy — the free gifts are mine to keep. I may preview each subsequent shipment for 15 days. If I don't want it, I simply return the books within 15 days and owe nothing. If I keep them I will pay just $12.50 (I save $2.50 off the retail price for 6 books) plus postage and handling and any applicable sales tax.

BRj

Prices subject to change. Orders subject to approval.

REMEMBER!

- The free books and gift are mine to keep!
- There is no obligation!
- I may preview each shipment for 15 days!
- I can cancel anytime!

(DETACH AND MAIL CARD TODAY!)

BUSINESS REPLY MAIL

FIRST-CLASS MAIL   PERMIT NO. 2456   HICKSVILLE, N.Y.

POSTAGE WILL BE PAID BY ADDRESSEE

Loveswept

Bantam Books
P.O. Box 985
Hicksville, NY 11802-9827

NO POSTAGE
NECESSARY
IF MAILED
IN THE
UNITED STATES

Lucy bobbed a head on which was wound a scraggly, white-blond braid. She grabbed the wax, darted a look at Sara from behind thick glasses, and hurried away, her skinny legs flapping inside ancient bell-bottom jeans.

Kyle came to get a drink of water, and to watch Sara polish colorful panes of glass set in a star pattern in the dining room windows. She glanced at him and was caught in the mesmerizing closeness of his solemn blue eyes. "Yes?"

"You won't let anyone else onto the grounds," he said, frowning, "but you trust Tom and Lucy, and they're two of the strangest characters I've ever seen."

"My mother hired them while I was . . . you know."

"In Surador?" His stern expression gentled at her continuing discomfort over mentioning that part of her life.

"Yes. When I came home she told me she'd been giving Tom and Lucy odd jobs to do and that they'd never caused her a minute's worry. Mother was a great judge of people, and she'd decided that they were exactly what they appeared to be—poor, simple, and straight out of a little coal-mining town somewhere way back in the hills." Sara shrugged lightly. "They've never done anything to make me think otherwise."

At that moment Tom broke into a shuffling sort of clog, dancing in the leaves like a carefree scarecrow. Clothed in patched overalls and a military fatigue shirt, lanky black hair flopping along his shoulders, he pumped his arms up and down merrily. Inside the boundaries of an angular face his mouth opened in a wide smile. He had a bad overbite accented by three gold-capped teeth. After a minute he quit dancing and went back to raking.

"I've conducted business in backwoods places where there were some pretty odd people," Kyle commented dryly. "But this guy would draw crowds in a zoo."

"You're awfully judgmental."

"I'm trying to understand what you see in Tom and Lucy that you didn't see in me. Why you don't bat an eyelash at letting two flaky locals inside the grounds once a week but you made *me* fight for entrance every inch of the way."

"They don't ask questions. They don't make demands."

"When you look at them you don't see an ugly past and an even uglier future," he retorted.

Reckless anger flared inside her. "Ugly, ugly, ugly," she chanted. "Is that what you are?"

He looked stunned. Then he said, "Hell, yes. At least I'm honest about it."

Without another word he walked out. Sara rested her forehead on a cool blue pane of glass and wished she hadn't been so quick to fight with him. Ever since his arrival at the keep she'd felt restless—she could describe it only as a sense of knowing how incomplete she'd been before she saw him again. In her whole life she'd never had to fight such a dangerous combination of devotion and desire.

The poignancy of it was frightening. In research terms, she'd finally found the known unknown, the piece missing from an equation. Now that he was part of her life, the equation was solved; she knew what she'd been looking for all along.

After Tom and Lucy collected their pay and drove off in a rattling, rusty old van, Sara offered to cook supper. She'd never had much success with cooking—she couldn't resist experimenting, which was a great attitude for the lab but a disastrous one for the kitchen. But this evening she wanted to do something to shock and please Kyle.

He, however, was not in the mood to appreciate her offer. Without being bad-tempered about it, he claimed *houseworkis bummed-outis*, which was, he assured her, a temporary form of exhaustion suffered by macho men. Then he filled a tray with pineapple and cheese sandwiches, potato chips, and two of his beloved Coco-Moos.

He carried it to his room, along with a stack of old Zane Grey westerns he'd gotten from one of the castle's many bookcases. Sara felt like crying as he disappeared into his bedroom and shut the door. He was hurt, though he'd probably never admit it.

She didn't know what to call her feelings for him. The word *love* kept surfacing, but it was always accompanied by a sense of despair, so she tried not to think about it. She and Kyle were still strangers in so many ways. But everything, *everything* about him fascinated her.

At times he was as wholesome as a box of corn flakes, but there was always the underlying glint in his eye, the worldly look that fit the things he'd told her about himself during their shared meals.

She would never forget the day she had talked to him in Valdivia's courtyard. He had told her and Dinah, in a businesslike tone, that he would kill Valdivia if he had to. Since he was chained helplessly to a large stone fountain, he'd made that threat with a smile, poking fun at the irony of his own bravado. But Sara had not doubted that he meant every word, that he had the training and the inclination to kill Valdivia, and, from the look in his eyes, that he wouldn't lose any sleep over it if he did.

That was the kind of hatred he still felt for Valdivia. For Noelle's father.

Seven

Sara had no appetite. She went to the nursery, fed Noelle, and read to her from a science journal. Noelle squealed and gurgled her appreciation for her mother's voice, even if the subject was ectotrophic and endotrophic types of mycorrhizal associations. Daisy fell asleep on the floor by Sara's rocking chair, snoring softly, paws to the ceiling.

Noelle refused to yawn, blink slowly, or give any other sign that she was getting sleepy. "I have work to do, petunia," Sara said mildly. Finally Sara carried her downstairs to the greenhouse and put her in an extra playpen she kept there.

"Snoot," Noelle said happily, welcoming the big toy elephant that lived in the playpen. She stood up and put her arms around his head, then began to talk in her mysterious baby language of noises and half words. Daisy flopped down in the sawdust beside the playpen.

Sara watched the cheerful scene for a second, then turned blindly and grabbed the dirt-stained apron she wore when she worked in the greenhouse. Her fingers shook as she slipped the yoke of it over her head. She feared the worst about tomorrow. Kyle was on the verge of forcing her to spend time outside the keep. She had to think of new excuses.

Sara went down the long rows of tables, making notes on the charts that hung from the table edges at regular intervals, checking moisture levels, studying leaf development, and weeding out weak and dying plants. At heart she was simply a gardener. She loved to work with the plants in the greenhouse, getting her hands covered in the damp, fertile soil, smelling the rich scents of the flowers, and watching the endless variations grow into fascinating forms. Even without the added pleasure of sunshine and fresh air, gardening brought her into sync with a peaceful world.

Tonight, with the Lexington trip looming over her, she didn't know if she'd ever feel peaceful again.

Even while lost in thought about tomorrow, she automatically glanced up to check on Noelle occasionally. The baby sat with a collection of stacking rings between her feet. She kept trying to fit them over the end of Snoot's trunk.

Sara lost track of time, and when she finally glanced at her watch, ten minutes had passed. Smiling giddily, she lifted her head to check on Noelle. At the other end of the cavern, near the end of the long tables, the playpen sat empty.

"Noelle!"

Dark terror swept through Sara as she ran through the big greenhouse. Daisy was gone too. It didn't make sense. Noelle was as active as a small monkey these days, but she couldn't have gotten out of the playpen without help. Sara groaned out loud when she realized that Snoot now lay facedown, his big gray body mashed against the playpen's webbed side. He was just the right size to make a very effective ladder to the top.

Sara couldn't see beyond the greenery that covered the tables. When she reached the playpen she slid to a stop, looking around wildly. Noelle sat in the sawdust under the end of a table. She had managed to reach up and pull a knotty, twisted little vine from its pot. Daisy stood beside her, looking worried. Noelle was gleefully chewing a mouthful of the plant's soft, blue-black leaves.

And they were deadly.

Kyle sat up in bed, listening to the sound of doors slamming and feet running. He threw his book on the rumpled covers and went to the door quickly. As he jerked it open he heard Daisy bark furiously, then a crash, the sound of glass breaking. It came from down the hall. Sara's suite.

Kyle stepped outside his room as one of her double doors slammed open. She ran into the hall and halted, staring at him with wild, frightened eyes. She wore a dirty brown apron. Cradled to her chest she held a large bundle wrapped in the coverlet from her bed.

"What—" he began.

"Get your car!" She shivered visibly. To his amazement, the bundle under the coverlet moved a little.

"Sara, what—"

"*Get your car.* I have to go to the hospital!"

Whatever her problem, he'd ask questions later. Kyle stepped into his room only long enough to grab his wallet and keys, then jam his feet into his running shoes. By the time he ran out she was in the castle's foyer. She cried silently as she struggled to hold on to the mysterious something in her arms and unlock the massive door at the same time.

"Easy," he said, taking the key from her.

"Hurry, please hurry." Her voice was ragged, unrecognizable, her expression utterly distraught.

He pulled the door open. "Wait at the end of the bridge. I'll be right back." Thank God, the bridge was down. Kyle raced across it, then headed around back, where he'd parked the sports car. A minute later he jerked the car to a stop beside her, already opening the passenger door as she reached for the handle.

She slid into the front seat. Daisy, whining with an odd sound of fear, crowded inside by her feet. The interior lights revealed nothing of her puzzling bundle, because she still had the coverlet pulled over its head, top, or whatever, like a hood. Sara slammed the door, and crisp autumn darkness covered her mystery.

Kyle signaled the gate to open and barely gave it time to clear before the car hurtled through. "Hurry," Sara begged.

"Give me directions to the hospital."

"Go back to the main highway. Take a left. It's fifteen minutes from here."

"I'll make it in less than that."

After they left the driveway and hit the paved road of the national park, Kyle floored the accelerator and devoted all his concentration to driving. Years of experience with frantic and dangerous situations had taught him the folly of trying to do more than one risky thing at a time, so right now his only concern was driving as fast and as safely as he could.

Dimly he was aware of Sara pulling the coverlet back and touching whatever lay inside, of Sara trying not to sob and sounding even more distraught because of her efforts.

The mountain highway was nearly deserted and, except for a few sharp curves, easy to negotiate. Kyle glanced at the speedometer once and saw that it was tilted all the way to the right. He felt a boyish thrill of satisfaction. Those high school years when he and Jeopard had raced stock cars on dirt tracks in Florida had not been wasted.

The county hospital sat on a hill above a tiny town with one traffic light, which Kyle ran. He began to feel a delayed rush of adrenaline as he swung the car up to the hospital's emergency entrance. Soon he'd get some answers. He had a feeling that he was about to learn a great deal about Sara's mysterious lab work. What kind of animal/plant thing had she created back there? Frankenflower? The bright light of the hospital's emergency entrance filled the car.

Kyle leapt out and reached the passenger side by the time Sara shoved the door open. "Let me." He grabbed for her so quickly that she was startled. Kyle pulled the strange bundle from her arms and into his.

"No!"

"Shh, Sara. Whatever it is—" His voice died as the coverlet fell open. Kyle stared down at a beautiful dark-haired baby who seemed to be asleep. Shock poured through him.

Sara vaulted from the car, grabbed the baby, and ran for the hospital doors.

"Well, I have a simple diagnosis," the doctor told Sara finally, studying the long graph that the electro-cardiogram had just produced. "She must have just swallowed a fraction of that plant, because all it's done is make her go sound asleep. Her vital signs are a little sluggish, but normal."

Sara sagged against the end of the examining table. She kept the fingertips of one hand against Noelle's head, reassuring herself with the warmth of Noelle's scalp. She felt Kyle's hand, strong and comforting, against the small of her back. "I couldn't tell if she'd swallowed any or not," Sara murmured wearily. "But I knew that even one leaf would have . . ." She couldn't finish that thought.

Kyle slid his arm around her. "What now?" he asked the doctor.

As a nurse removed the electrodes that were taped to Noelle's chest, the pudgy, friendly looking doctor grinned, happy to give good news. "We'll just keep her overnight, for observation. You and your wife can stay with her if you want."

"All right," Kyle told the man. "We will."

For the first time in an hour Sara took her eyes away from her daughter's small, still form, clad only in a diaper. She looked at Kyle dully. His eyes were somber but not angry. Not angry yet, anyway, she thought with a stab of despair. He would demand the truth.

The nurse started to pick up Noelle. "I'll take her," Sara said urgently, reaching out.

The nurse shook her head but smiled. "You're a nervous wreck, Mom. I'm just going to transfer her to something with wheels on it, so we can take her upstairs. Hospital policy."

Sara dogged the nurse's steps as she took Noelle to a gurney. The nurse got a blanket. "Here, Mom. You do the tucking. I'll send an orderly in a minute."

Now, as the frantic atmosphere calmed down, everyone left Sara and Kyle alone with Sara's secret, a secret no more. She covered Noelle with the blanket, then bent over her with a convulsive little shiver. Wrapping her arms around the baby, she put her head next to Noelle's and cried, partially from relief over her safety but also from the torment of knowing that she could no longer protect Noelle or Kyle from the truth.

She felt his hand caress her hair. "She'll be fine, Sara," he said, his voice low and troubled.

"Thank you. Thank you for helping me get her here so fast."

"You didn't have to keep her hidden from me."

"Yes, I did."

"Why?"

The orderly came over, and her presence effectively ended the conversation. Not until thirty minutes later, when Noelle was settled in a crib in a tiny private room, Daisy had been coaxed into keeping the hospital's security guard company for the night, and Sara's hands were steady enough to hold a cup of coffee without spilling any, did Kyle ask the question again.

The hospital was small, only half full, and informal; the room was in an adult ward, since pediatrics was low on both patients and nurses that night. Sara and Kyle sat on the bed, their legs dangling off the side. He looked at her grimly. "Why couldn't you tell me about your baby?"

Sara stared into the crib and curled her hands tighter around the plastic coffee cup. "I didn't want *anyone* to know about her," she explained wearily. "So no one from our government or any other government could use her to force me into cooperation." She paused. "The way I was used to force *my* mother."

Kyle squeezed her knee. "Sara, what happened with Valdivia was a fluke. He was a lone wolf, a renegade. Even the Soviets didn't care for him too much. No one else is going to bother you."

She looked at Kyle warily, her nerves frayed. "What do you mean, what happened with . . . with Valdivia? What do you think happened?"

"Shh. Calm down. I mean your kidnapping. The forced research."

"Oh." Her shoulders sagged. Another minute's reprieve.

Kyle slid a hand across the nape of her neck and massaged gently. "You told the doctor that Noelle is ten months old. Even a non-genius like me can figure out that she was born eight or nine months after you were rescued in Surador."

"Yes." Sara gazed into her coffee, feeling a blackness that matched its color.

"I think I can guess what happened."

She almost cracked her coffee cup. "Go ahead."

"There were a lot of rebel soldiers involved in the rescue. Young, idealistic, courageous—and they liked Americans." Kyle chuckled ruefully. "Surador is one of the few countries in South America where *anyone* likes us. You were in shock. I know that from my brother's report. Especially after he told you that Valdivia had committed suicide."

Sara nodded, her heart racing. What was he getting at?

"It's only human to need comfort in a situation like that," Kyle continued, his hand stroking her neck, his voice soothing. "And there must have been a soldier who wanted to offer it. You didn't have the ability, at that moment, to think about the consequences." He paused, then gestured slowly toward the crib. "Nine months later you gave birth to those consequences."

Sara bit her lower lip until it throbbed. She shut her eyes, trying desperately to judge the wild possibility whirling through her mind. Would it work? It *could.* Why not? How would anyone ever learn the truth?

You'd be living another lie, telling another lie to Kyle. You don't want that, do you?

I'll live any lie if it will keep him and Noelle from being hurt by what Valdivia did.

Sara swallowed harshly. Then she looked directly into Kyle's sympathetic blue eyes. She knew then, as goose bumps ran down her spine and a precious new hope began to burn inside her, that she had a chance to offer him love, to help him chase away his own dragons. The chance was worth the lie.

"I can't believe how much insight you have," she whispered. "It's incredible."

"I'm right?"

She nodded. For a fleeting second she felt guilty over his compassion. Then she reminded herself that this deception would spare him a great deal of heartache. Tentatively she asked, "Do you think I was wrong to keep Noelle?"

"You obviously could have chosen not to keep her, but you didn't. And you're obviously crazy about her.

So why would I think there was anything wrong about it?"

She managed to smile. "Because I think you and I were raised the same way—to expect Mommy to marry Daddy before she has a baby."

"I expect Mommy to live in the real world, where it's not always so simple."

Her heart nearly burst with devotion for him. "We unwed mommies of the world salute you."

"I still don't understand why you just couldn't tell me—or anyone else—about Noelle. Were you *that* afraid for her safety?"

"Yes." That much was true, though not for the reason he thought. Any link to Valdivia would bring a horde of government investigators down on her. Their suspicions might lead to some kind of incriminating circumstantial evidence. What if they tried to charge her with conspiracy, or treason? What if they tried to take Noelle away?"

"What now, Tinker Bell?"

"I suppose I'll start learning to trust the outside world again. If you'll help me."

The slow, wide smile that spread across his mouth took her breath away, and she was reassured that her deception, if it held up, would be the most loving thing she could do for him.

Reality had not seemed quite so real last night, Kyle thought grimly. He woke up as he had gone to sleep—lying on the hospital bed, fully clothed. The only difference was that Sara was no longer curled up beside him. As bright morning sunshine caressed her, she bent over the crib and spoke quietly to her daughter. He heard Noelle's sleepy cooing, in return.

He watched the sweet, gentle scene and his throat closed with emotion. How would Sara feel about having him around Noelle? He didn't doubt that the child was going to scream every time she saw his face. Sara might be able to deal with his scars, but he wondered how she'd deal with the fact that the sight of him would terrify her daughter?

"Oh, I see that crabby morning expression of yours," Sara murmured to the baby, and smiled so tenderly that Kyle couldn't take his eyes away from the beautiful, tormenting sight. "Are you hungry? The doctor says that I can feed you if you are."

Kyle had a sudden mental image of the baby nursing at one of Sara's breasts. He'd seen women nurse before, but never *his* woman and *his* baby, which was, despite the swift mental kick he gave himself, the way he thought of Sara and Noelle.

Kyle cleared his throat. "I'll come back when you're finished."

She looked startled. "Good morning."

He got up off the far side of the bed and casually maneuvered toward the door, hoping that Noelle was still groggy and wouldn't notice him. "I'll come back," he repeated.

Sara laughed, to his relief, appearing happier and more relaxed than he'd ever seen her before. Telling him about the baby had done her a lot of good. "You look as if you expect a raid from the vice squad," she teased. She touched her denim shirt. "I bet that if I started undoing buttons, you'd run."

He wagged his finger at her. "I never run from an unbuttoned woman."

"Well, relax, Surprise. I don't breastfeed."

Kyle leaned against a wall near the door, making certain that he was standing where Noelle couldn't crane her head and see him easily. Already she was waving her arms and looking around. "Oh? Why not?"

"It hurt too much each time I boiled my nipples." When he looked at her blankly, not quite certain why anyone would boil nipples, their own or otherwise, she laughed again. "I can see that you know as little about feeding babies as I did." She smiled, her green eyes alight with affection. "That's all right. To answer your question, I didn't have enough milk to make the effort worth Noelle's trouble. So after a couple of months of dedicated misery for both of us, I started giving her a bottle."

He shook his head. "A scientist *and* an expert mother. Now when I talk to you I can feel ignorant on two levels."

"Believe me, being a scientist came easier to me than being a mother. I always trusted facts rather than instincts. But now that I've got the hang of motherhood, I think my instincts are pretty reliable."

"I'd say they're terrific."

She blushed with pleasure. "Would you like to be introduced to Noelle?"

"Later."

Her eyes clouded. "Is anything wrong?"

"Nah. I just thought I'd go down to the security guard's office and check on Daisy. She might have fallen asleep and been mistaken for a doorstop during the night."

"All right, but come here and say hello first." She reached into the crib, her eyes gleaming with pride as she studied the baby. Slowly she lifted Noelle out. "She's not quite herself, so don't expect any smiles yet. Kyle? Kyle?"

He had already left the room.

Sara's confusion and worry grew when he waited an hour before returning—and came back then only after sending a nurse's aide to make certain that Noelle was napping. He strode in quickly, looking brusque and formal even though he was still dressed in yesterday's sweat pants and a faded football jersey.

"Daisy survived the night," he announced, "but two doctors and a lab technician were hypnotized watching her sleep. They're lying on their backs on the floor, snoring, with their arms and legs in the air. It's not a pretty sight."

Sitting on the bed, Sara shifted Noelle in her arms and was dismayed to see him take a step back, as if wary. "She is asleep, isn't she?" he asked.

"Yes, Kyle," she answered, frowning.

"I've taken care of the checkout process. As soon as a nurse comes to wheel Noelle downstairs, we can leave. I thought I'd let you and the baby have the back seat of the car, and I'll put Daisy in the front with me."

"Does your car have a trunk? Noelle and I could sit in there if you're really ashamed to be seen with us."

He looked so stunned and then so apologetic that she regretted her barb. "I'm not ashamed," he said hotly.

"Then what is it?"

"Nothing." Noelle stirred, yawned, and rubbed her eyes. "I'll be downstairs in the car," he said, abruptly leaving the room.

When they returned to the keep he went to the kitchen to fix a late breakfast.

"I've unlocked the doors to the back," Sara told him after she had finished settling Noelle in her crib. "You're welcome to come see the lab, the greenhouse, and the nursery too. If you're interested."

He studiously pushed strips of bacon around on a griddle. Sara noted that his bacon was laid out in neat, orderly rows. It was military bacon, a sign of an organized mind. When she cooked bacon she usually spent too much time trying to see where it cooked fastest in the pan, or which end curled first, or how the amount of shrinkage related to the heat of the stove. Usually she ended up with burned bacon.

"I'd like to see the lab and greenhouse," he told her.

But not Noelle's nursery. Sara sat down at the table and watched him carefully. He was either worried about Noelle's reaction to his scars, or he wasn't too pleased to have a baby around in general. There was one way to find out.

"I'll be back in a minute," she said pleasantly.

"Not too long. I'm scrambling the eggs right now."

By the time she returned, carrying Noelle, he was dumping the finished eggs on a plate. He pivoted, saw the baby staring at him, and froze.

Her heart in her throat, Sara glanced at Noelle's equally startled eyes and prayed for good results. "Kyle, meet Noelle. Noelle, meet Kyle. Ky-ul."

The coaching over the past few days paid off. Noelle's head bobbed toward Sara, then back toward Kyle. "Cal," she said distinctly.

Sara tried to smile despite the tension Kyle radiated. "Congratulations," she quipped. "Your name is now Cal. Don't feel bad. My name is Mop. At least yours is flattering."

"She's going to cry."

Sara glanced at Noelle's puckering mouth. "Probably. Later on she'll also soil her diapers, throw her toys, and argue when I try to get her to take a nap. All perfectly typical of a day in the life of a baby. It won't have anything to do with her like or dislike for you."

"Cal," Noelle said again, with more emphasis. She reached out with a small hand, curling her fingers at him.

"Why is she doing that?" he demanded. "Look, she's getting teary."

He was right. The tears slid down her cheeks. She turned her head and burrowed into Sara's shoulder. With sinking hopes Sara watched Kyle's expression stiffen into a mask. Only his eyes revealed his humiliation and sorrow.

"I can pretty much guarantee that it won't get any better than it is right now," he said grimly.

"I think you're wrong," Sara said. "But for now we'll drop the subject." She turned to leave the room.

Noelle was now crying softly, making tired little noises. But her hand shot out over Sara's back, toward Kyle. "Cal!" she called plaintively.

Sara swiveled back to face Kyle. "She wants you or something you've got. Since you're a stranger, I suspect 'Cal' refers to scrambled eggs. Why don't you bring her a spoonful?"

"And see her retreat completely?"

"No, that only seems to be what you're doing."

"Yow. That went right to the heart."

He got a teaspoon and jabbed it into the pile of eggs. Slowly he advanced toward Noelle, the spoon clasped tightly in his big, nimble fingers. Noelle stared at him without blinking, without breathing.

"I feel as if I'm watching a lion tamer trying to sneak up on a lion," Sara teased gently. "Kyle, you look as if you think she might roar."

"She might," he said in a tense, hushed voice.

She opened her mouth, but only to accept the eggs. In her usual fashion she ate half and let half decorate her lower lip. His fingers trembling, Kyle wiped her mouth. She pursed her lips at him in gratitude and made a smacking sound. She held out her arms.

Sara's throat burned with tears. "She wants to give you a kiss. Do you mind?"

"Are you sure that's what she wants?"

"She might ask for a date later. But I think you're safe."

He moved closer by inches, alert for any sign that Noelle was going to recoil the second she discovered that he didn't look like other people. Sara realized that until today Noelle had seen very few people besides herself and her mother. For all Noelle knew, every man had funny lines and ridges on his face. And what girl, of any age, could resist Kyle's big blue eyes?

He placed his face within kissing range. Noelle grabbed his hair with both hands and planted a tiny, soft pucker on his cheek. A look of wonder came into his eyes. "Can I hold her?" he asked hoarsely.

"Of course. But don't be upset if she doesn't like it. You're a stranger."

A beloved one, apparently. Noelle put her arms around his neck and sat very still inside the crook of his elbow. His face, perhaps because it was unusual, mesmerized her. She gave him a sudden smile, bright, dimpled, and totally unafraid. And then she kissed him right on one of his scars, like a tiny enchantress releasing him from an evil spell.

Sara put her head on his shoulder and looked away so that he could stop fighting the moonlight that shimmered in his eyes.

Eight

For the rest of the day he and Noelle were inseparable. He carried her around the castle, listening solemnly while she described things in terms no one but another baby might understand. He helped feed her and laughed when she threw stewed apple at him. He read Zane Grey to her. He held her while she slept.

And the whole time Sara said silent prayers of thanks and other prayers that this was just the beginning of a dream so wonderful that nothing could ever destroy it. She watched Kyle with so much love that she knew he couldn't help but notice; she floated effortlessly through the day in a haze of affection and desire and finely tuned anticipation.

As a chilly mooncast autumn night settled around the keep, they built a fire in the great room. The smell of it permeated the castle with a cozy feeling of comfort and happiness. In the kitchen Kyle fixed dinner while Noelle babbled at him from her high chair and Sara simply sat at the kitchen table, smiling.

Afterwards they sat on the couch in front of the fire and quietly watched Noelle pester Daisy. "I never thought I'd like dogs again," Kyle murmured. "But I guess Daisy's unique. She's not a dog. She's an ottoman that slobbers."

Sara wanted to slide close to him on the couch, but she sensed some reserve. It wasn't going to be easy for him to relax, to believe that she saw so much more than the scars when she looked at him. She smiled and sipped from a mug of cider laced with brandy, confident that everything would work out.

"I didn't want a dog," she told Kyle. "I didn't want anything to remind me of that day in the courtyard. But Daisy was so opposite from those monsters. She reminded me of the good that balances all the bad."

"Not all of it," he corrected her, frowning thoughtfully into his own mug. "But enough."

"Noelle is a balance."

"Yes." His expression softened. "You're right about that. She's your best revenge."

"My what?"

"The compensation for what Valdivia put you through. The only good thing that came out of the situation. Do you understand what I'm saying? Because you were in Surador and you met Noelle's father, you have a wonderful little girl." He hesitated, then said grimly, "No. I'm sorry I put it that way. I won't give Valdivia *any* credit for bringing Noelle into the world. I don't even like to think of the bastard being indirectly responsible for you having her."

Sara squirmed inwardly. "He, uhmmm, he was a complex man," she said haltingly, weighing each word. "Sadistic, self-centered, arrogant—and yet he was capable of a twisted sort of love. He was obsessed with Dinah. I'm sure you read that in Jeopard's report."

"Yeah. Apparently his only regret was that he couldn't make her return the feeling. She was lucky that he didn't force her into a relationship. It was ironic that he had a sort of honor where she was concerned."

"She was lucky," Sara agreed, swallowing a knot of

emotion in her throat. She desperately wanted to say, *I wasn't.*

Kyle stared into the fire, his mouth set in a harsh line. "I have to admit something that may sound cynical to you. I'm glad that he was obsessed with Dinah. I know that he frightened her, and of course I'm glad that he didn't do anything worse, but . . . better her than you."

"You're not cynical. Just honest."

Sara shuddered with a rising tide of anguish that did nothing to make her want Kyle less. She needed to be reborn in his arms, to have his tenderness and his body make her forget the last time she'd been touched by a man. It hurt that she couldn't tell Kyle everything about her and Valdivia. *Everything* was a long, humiliating story that had begun years before the kidnapping, before she'd learned exactly what kind of man Diego de Valdivia was.

"Time for your bath," she said abruptly, knowing that she couldn't sit any longer and act casual.

"Do I get a rubber duck for the tub?" Kyle asked, amused and startled. "Will you wash behind my ears?"

Sara forced a laugh as she went to pick Noelle up. "I was referring to your friend here. But you're welcome to be my assistant. Just prepare to be splashed."

He rose and came over to them, frowning a little. "James Bond was never confronted by domestic life. I'll tell you what. Let's all go take baths—in different bathrooms."

"All right. Would you like to rendezvous in the nursery in thirty minutes?"

He drew himself up and gave her a playful salute. "Mission accepted."

Kyle found her in the nursery tucking a pink blanket around Noelle, who lay in the crib with one small arm around a toy bear. "Hi," she whispered, her eyes glancing briefly over the burgundy robe that hung untied over his white T-shirt and burgundy jogging pants. "You're color coordinated," she noted, and turned her attention back to Noelle.

"Sophistication is my middle name." He sighed. "It isn't easy being this debonair."

He stood at the foot of the crib, his eyes taking in Sara's soft blue robe and the white sweatshirt that showed above the loosely belted waist. Her hair was damp and tousled from the bath; she smelled of lemon soap. Her face had a fresh-scrubbed blush, and the elfin features, set in a gentle, slightly pensive expression, were heart-stopping.

His body pulsed with the sight and scent of her, and his reaction caused him to close and tie his robe. Cotton jogging pants didn't hide a man's thoughts very well. When Sara glanced at his actions, he muttered, "It's cool in here."

She checked a thermostat on the wall. "Seventy-three degrees."

"In Florida we call that cool."

Even as every impulse strained with desire for her, his more rational observations told him the truth. She wasn't dressed to seduce or be seduced; she was dressed to be friendly, comfortable, and unappealing. She failed miserably at being unappealing. He glanced down at her feet. She was wearing the silly slippers with tiger faces on them. He had to give her credit. Without speaking a word, she was kindly telling him no.

Today he'd begun to think that a future was opening up for them. Maybe it would, in time. But not tonight. He realized that he was stroking one finger across a scar on the opposite hand. The scars were always there, always taunting.

"Kyle?" He pulled himself from his painful reverie as Sara straightened, gazing at him worriedly. "Are you okay?"

"Sure." He gestured jauntily at the room. "I'm just not accustomed to so much pink."

"You know, sometimes you get a look in your eyes that reminds me of your brother. As if everything just froze over. It's deadly cold."

He smiled sardonically. "I use it to frighten small animals and little old ladies."

"Cal," Noelle's sleepy voice called. She made a smacking sound.

"I can tell that it works," Sara said, smiling. She stepped aside. "You've terrified this baby bunny, as you can see."

He sighed with pleasure as he moved around the crib. Noelle held up the hand that wasn't clutching her toy. A giggle ended in another comical pursing of her lips. He bent down and kissed her on the tip of the nose. She returned the favor, then yawned.

"I'm insulted," he quipped.

Daisy stretched out on her dog pillow under the crib. Sara turned the lights off, leaving only a night-light that cast a warm yellow glow. Kyle stepped from the room as she kissed her daughter good night, murmuring soft words that seemed to deserve privacy. He would have given anything to believe that someday he might be included in the love between them.

She left the door open and walked into a shadowed hallway where modern carpeting and light fixtures contrasted with stone walls and medieval decor. A narrow hallway led off it—the secret passage to her bedroom, he knew now. Another led to the lab and the staircase that went into the greenhouse below.

She pointed toward that hallway. "Come with me." Silently he followed her to the wide stone stairway. The stones were cold on his bare feet as he descended behind Sara. She opened a steel security door. "I want to get something from the greenhouse. I thought you'd like to look around."

He followed her into a world of great warmth and ripe, earthy scents that made him remember the hot aroma of a Florida marsh. The cavern was a jungle—an organized jungle, with charts and tables and clinical-looking cubicles whose translucent walls seemed to glow from the lights within. Parrots fluttered across the ceiling; insects hummed.

"Eden underground," Kyle said, awed. "What kind of plants are you growing here?"

"Rare ones—at least, rare in terms of our knowledge of them. They're from the rain forest. No one has studied them before. There are still hundreds of plant species waiting to be discovered—if we don't destroy the forest first. The other problem is that the Indian tribes who know how to use these plants are all dying out or giving up their traditions. We're losing the last generation of medicine men who can tell us what miracles these plants might produce."

"Miracles?"

"Medicine. Like the liniment I gave you for your back. Like cures for everything from cancer to the common cold." She paused, looking hesitant, then added softly, "And something that I want to try on you tonight. If you don't mind."

He put his hands on his hips and arched a brow in mild defiance. "Do I look like a guinea pig?"

She grinned. "We'll discuss your species orientation later. Look, what I have in mind won't hurt you, I'm certain. I can't promise that it will produce any dramatic results, but it would be interesting to experiment with. I've tried it on myself, so I know that it's safe."

"Okay, I'm fearless—or at least too dumb to say no. What is it?"

She pushed up the sleeve of her robe and pointed to a small white scar on her forearm. "I got this twenty years ago when I played 'Two Musketeers' with my brother, using a couple of swords from my grandfather's collection. This scar used to be much more noticeable."

Kyle grabbed her arm and studied the innocuous white line intensely. "What did you put on it?"

"Can you stand to smell like an orchid?"

"I can stand to smell like a swamp if it makes my scars look better."

She laughed. "Good. It won't change them overnight, and it won't make them go away. But it may fade them, especially the smaller ones." She took Kyle's hand and led him through the greenhouse to one of the glowing cubicles. Inside were racks of brilliantly colored orchids, smaller and more fragile than any American variety he'd ever seen. The flowers had the delicate beauty of butterfly wings.

She plucked the blooms from several plants. "Now we go up to the kitchen and make a facial with these and a little milk." She smiled at him puckishly. "I *knew* I'd find a reason to use my blender someday."

Upstairs she turned the orchid blooms into flecks of bright color in a milky froth. Carrying a hand towel, she nodded toward the great room, where the fire still burned high enough to provide light.

"The easiest way to do this would be for you to stretch out on the rug. Take off your robe. I'll do your face and arms."

Any worries Kyle had about the effect of her touch were momentarily forgotten in his intrigue over the orchids. He removed the robe, stretched out with his head on a big throw pillow and, just to be on the careful side, jumbled the robe over his belly and thighs.

She sat down beside him, holding the blender. "Shut your eyes."

He did as she asked, but couldn't resist warning, "If this potion turns me into a dandelion, I'm going to sue you, Doc."

"But you'll have great petals." Chuckling, she began to spread the cool mixture on his face.

Kyle flinched inwardly at the feel of her fingertips exploring his scars, but his slight discomfort couldn't destroy other, more compelling responses. Within a minute he was very glad that he'd covered himself with the robe.

"I'm trying to massage the liquid into the scar tissue," she explained softly as her fingers stroked the ugly ridge across his nose.

"Other than myself and my plastic surgeon, you're the first person who's touched my face."

Her voice dropped, becoming husky. "That's too bad. It's such a nice face."

"No compliments, all right?" he said. "I don't believe them, and I don't expect them."

After a second she agreed wearily, "No compliments." Her fingers moved to one of his arms. She rubbed the liquid into it from elbow to hand. Then, as if the small scar on his palm required an inordinate amount of attention, she took her time stroking it.

Kyle shifted his legs, feeling the caress in areas that had little to do with his palm. She performed the same magic on the other hand, and he used all his concentration to keep from moving in an even more noticeable way.

"It's too damned warm in front of this fire," he grumbled, breathing faster. "Floor's hard." The floor wasn't the only thing that fit that description, he thought. He arched his back a little and drew his knees up.

"Be still," she cautioned. "This stuff has to dry for a minute or two. Then you can move. In the meantime" —she tugged his T-shirt up to his nipples—"I'll use the rest of the mixture."

Kyle could barely keep from groaning as her fingers spread over his chest and stomach, massaging the liquid into the scars there. One scar ran across his right nipple, and when her fingertip slid over the sensitive nub, Kyle bit the inside of his lip to stifle a growl of encouragement.

Her fingers glided along a ragged scar at the center of his chest, tracing without inhibition a path that he knew so well, had studied with loathing so many times. The scar bore an uncanny resemblance to a V; it looked as if Valdivia's dogs had left his personal brand near Kyle's heart.

Sara's touch made his skin tingle as if a grid of high-voltage wires lay just under the surface. No other woman's touch had ever had such an incredible effect, bringing the heat of desire and emotion to the surface until his control was weakened with each stroke of her fingers.

Because his skin had become a supersenitive canvas for her magical art, the warm, foreign drop of water that fell on his stomach was an abrupt intrusion. Kyle opened his eyes quickly and looked at her. She was crying as she looked at his torso. One of her tears had fallen on him. *Pity.* He died a little as embarrassment crawled through him. "Stop it."

Her startled gaze flew to his, and her lips parted on a soft murmur of apology. "You don't understand," she whispered.

"No tears. No damned tears."

She swallowed harshly and scrubbed her cheeks with the back of one hand, hurrying to comply. But she shook her head in rebuke. "Why won't you let me feel sorry for you? It's only human for me to cry when I think of what you went through. I *know* what happened to you after that day in the courtyard. I know that you were taken to another hacienda and treated like some sort of prisoner of war."

He cursed viciously. "Who told you about that?"

"Jeopard. When we were all at the hospital, going through the—what did your people call it? The debriefing. You wouldn't tell me *anything*, remember?"

"I didn't think you wanted to hear the details. I didn't think you could take it. There was something haunted about your eyes. Maybe you don't remember as well as I do. You avoided me most of the time at the hospital. Then you left without even telling me good-bye."

She looked at him sadly. "How could I face you after . . . being with Noelle's father?"

He groaned softly, a sound of regret and understanding. "I wouldn't have tried to make you feel guilty for that. You and I met only one time. When you were rescued you still didn't know that I had survived. I was no more than a dead stranger in your memory."

"A dead stranger?" She stared at him in disbelief. "I never thought of you that way!" Her shoulders slumped. "When I found out that you were alive but badly hurt, I assumed that you wouldn't want anything to do with me. After all, if you hadn't been assigned to find me . . ." She looked at him with the pain of memories in her eyes. "But after I saw you at the hospital, I *had* to know everything that had happened to you after that day in the courtyard. So I asked Jeopard."

"You shouldn't have."

She struggled for control and had to turn her face away. "I had to. You were so thin, and the scars . . . I could tell that your wounds had healed poorly. I asked Jeopard. He said that you'd been kept in a cellar, that you had never received any medical care, that some of the wounds had become infected."

Kyle sat up and grabbed the towel she'd brought. Roughly he began toweling her orchid concoction off his face and body.

"No," she said brokenly, reaching out to him, her hand shaking. "Please don't."

"When I want pity from you, I'll ask for it."

"You don't understand. My sympathy doesn't take anything away from all the good feelings that you and I share."

"It takes away a hell of a lot. Respect, for one thing." He knew that he was overreacting, that she was trying to be kind and he was kicking her for it. But he didn't want kindness from her—he wanted her to see him as a strong, desirable man, someone for whom she didn't have to feel sorry, someone she could love.

He got up. "Good night. I know I'm a bastard right now. I'll try to get my good humor back before breakfast."

Kneeling on the floor, she looked up at him, seeming small and fragile. But her eyes snapped with resentment. "You *are* a bastard right now," she agreed.

He bowed in acceptance, and left the room.

Sara sat there alone, her hands clenched in her lap, her thoughts rebellious. She had tried so hard to make him relax. Her unseductive attitude and conversation and the way she had dressed for bed had been meant to make intimacy seem so comfortable, so *right*. She had obviously taken the wrong approach.

She leapt to her feet and hurried from the room. First she went to her bedroom, where she kicked her tiger slippers into a corner, then stripped naked. She covered herself in the green silk robe she'd been wearing the day he had climbed down her chimney unannounced.

Next she went to the nursery, tiptoeing so that she wouldn't wake Noelle and Daisy. She rummaged through a set of drawers until she found everything she wanted. Her arms full, she went back to her bedroom, shoved open the door to the hall, and marched down to Kyle's room.

She used one bare heel to drum loudly on the bottom of his door. He apparently thought some new emergency had risen, because she heard him run to the door. He jerked it open and looked down at her worriedly. "What is it?"

"Respect," she said grimly, and found a knot in her throat. Why did he make this so difficult? "You want respect, I brought you respect."

He frowned at the things in her arms. As his eyes took in her change of clothes, he frowned harder. "Is this an experiment? Will there be a quiz later?"

"My mother liked to sew and crochet," she told him between gritted teeth. "She also did embroidery. Look." She threw one of Noelle's crib blankets at him.

He caught it, his angry, bewildered gaze never leaving hers. "Just tell me what point you're trying to make, Sara."

"I can't tell you. You don't listen. You don't believe." She nodded toward the blanket. "Look at it."

Slowly he dropped his gaze. His fingers touched a corner of the blanket where Anna Scarborough had embroidered her granddaughter's initials. "NKS," he read, then looked at her impatiently.

She threw a pink cap at him. "NKS," he said again, the cap spread over his hand as if his fingers were wearing it.

"NKS," she echoed, her voice trembling with bittersweet distress. She threw a tiny dress at him. Its collar bore the same initials. "NKS." She threw a pair of mittens. "NKS!" Then a monogrammed sweater. "NKS!"

"Whoa," he protested, trying to hold everything. When she drew her hand back with a pillow in it, like a powder-puff quarterback, he began to back away. "Easy, Sara, easy." His voice was soothing, his expression sad. "I'm sorry I upset you like this. Now, calm—"

"NKS!" She advanced into his room, her arm still posed to fire the pillow at him.

"Dammit!" he said finally, and stopped backing. He tossed everything on the floor and came toward her, hands out to grab the small pink pillow edged in crochet.

"NKS!" she yelled, and thrust the pillow into his hands.

Kyle halted, staring at the name that had been lovingly stitched into its center. "Noelle Kyla Scarborough," he whispered. "Kyla?"

Sara's anger crumbled. "I named her after you," she said, her voice breaking. "If that's not respect, I don't know what is."

He continued to look at the pillow, his blue eyes reflecting his stunned, troubled thoughts. "Why did you do it?"

"Because I wanted to honor the most wonderful man I'd ever met. Because I never wanted to forget that man." She stepped close to him and laid a hand on his arm. "Because from the first day I knew that he was very, very special." He brushed his fingertips over the name on the pillow. His hand quivered visibly, and his voice was hoarse.

"I hope I haven't done too much to destroy your opinion."

Her throat ached with emotion. "Nothing you can't fix easily."

He looked up at her, restraint and tenderness creating a volatile gleam in his eye. "Tell me what you want."

"I want you to show a little pity for *me.*"

"Oh, God, let's drop the subject of pity—"

"No." She took the baby pillow from him and tossed it onto a chair in his shadowy bedroom. Then she grasped his hands. "You can't bear the thought that I might feel sorry for you. But don't you feel sorry for me? For my loneliness? Don't you want to make me happy?"

"Any way that I can—"

"Then why won't you accept the fact that I want you?" She raised her hands and cupped his face. Sara watched the slow tensing of the muscles. "I love touching you," she whispered. "I love looking at you. And I'd love to do a great deal more of both."

He was silent, searching her eyes, his torn emotions evident in the tense set of his broad shoulders and the quiet dilemma that darkened his expression. *Give him time,* Sara told herself firmly.

Stepping back from him was one of the most difficult

things she'd ever done in her life. "I love you," she told him. She smiled through tears of hope. "I am going to believe that you want me to love you, and that eventually you'll believe that I do. In the meantime, I'll be waiting. Good night."

She turned shakily and started for the door. He reached it with a few loping strides and blocked her way. Sara gasped lightly as he snatched her into his arms and pulled her against him, lifting her to her toes.

"Would you say the first part again?" he said.

She lost herself in his hypnotizing gaze. "I love you, Kyle." Sara laughed weakly. "I think I knew that in Surador. We were strangers, but I knew that I wanted to be a part of you. How's that for jumping to an unsubstantiated, unscientific conclusion?"

"Sometimes you have to go with your instincts, Doc," he whispered, his voice deep and husky with emotion.

"Do you . . . do your instincts tell you anything specific?"

"They tell me that I was right that day in Surador."

She looked at him through half-shut eyes and wound her arms around his neck. "Right about what?"

"That I wouldn't mind dying for you."

Destroyed in the most tender way, she broke into a million pieces. Sara buried her head against the crook of his neck and cried.

"Oh, Sara, Sara," he said anxiously. "I was just being honest, not trying to upset you."

"That's why it means so much to me."

He managed to chuckle. "Do you know what else I was right about?"

"What?"

"This." He sank his mouth onto hers for a long, deep kiss that buckled her knees. "And this." He stroked his hands up and down her back, slid them over her hips, and pulled her tight against his pelvis. "I knew you'd be magic."

She gave herself to him, arching into his embrace, licking the corners of his mouth, then kissing the dampness she had made, whimpering with devotion each time he opened her lips with the loving command of his tongue.

He dipped his head and delved into the smooth flow of her neck, nuzzling the sensitive skin under her ear. Sensation scattered down Sara's body, and she curled into his arms as he lifted her from the floor. Kyle carried her down the hall to the master bedroom and stood quietly in the dim light from a single bedside lamp, kissing her until her head fell back weakly and she moaned.

"I thought you'd be more relaxed here," he whispered, laying her on the bed. He glanced at the open door to the nursery. "Where we could hear if Noelle cries during the night."

Looking up into the warm, unclouded blue of his gaze, Sara smiled. He understood so perfectly. She drew him down to her and nibbled his lower lip. "Thank you."

"Thank you." He slid a hand under her head and raised her face to be mapped by kisses. "Thank you." Slowly he settled beside her, his belly curved against her hip. He stroked the backs of his fingers down her robe and was superbly adept at raising goose bumps on the flesh underneath.

Again and again he repeated his patient caress from shoulder to thigh, and now he found points of particular interest, where he lingered, bonding the silk's smooth seduction with the more primitive urgency of his hand.

Sara writhed under his touch and kissed him wildly. Her hands tugged at his robe, pushed it open, and impatiently roamed over his T-shirt. She realized she was going too fast, being too greedy, and slowed her hands. Then, taking an infinite amount of joy in his clothed body, the hardness of his chest muscles, the slow flexing of his thighs under the cotton jogging pants, she met and held his gaze.

"I love you," he said in a tone that made her feel as if she were floating. "And I wish I were the man I see in your eyes."

"You are." She guided him onto his back and leaned over him, smiling tenderly. Sara knelt and ran her hands along his body, finding the special places as he had done with her body. When she caressed the straining ridge on his belly, he made a soft growl that was potently masculine.

She began to push his shirt up. He grasped her hands and burned her with a pensive, questioning look. "Would you like to turn out the light?"

She shook her head gently. "Would you?"

"Not really. I want to see you. I just wasn't certain—"

"I do," she answered. "I want to see you too. All of you. You have to understand something. I think you're the sexiest man I've ever known. When you did that ridiculous striptease for my security cameras, I was enthralled. I mean that."

He laughed, the kind of rich, relieved sound that told her she'd finally started to break through. Slowly the laughter faded into a look that simmered with desire. "Would you like a second performance?"

She nodded eagerly and even applauded a little.

Kyle rose from the bed and moved a few feet away, his back to her, the glow of the bedside lamp casting him in a tantalizing mixture of light and shadow. He shrugged his robe off one shoulder, struck a melodramatic pose with one hip thrust out, then smoothed both hands over his hair in a preening gesture.

He swiveled a little and let the robe fall from the other shoulder. With the burgundy material draped around his elbows, he pulled it back and forth across his rump.

"More, more," Sara urged, laughing softly. But this was no bawdy performance, this was a sharing of trust.

He dropped the robe and turned around. One brow arched wickedly as he splayed his hands across his stomach and rubbed, inviting her to think about the terraced muscles under his T-shirt.

Sara pressed her hands to her throat and sighed grandly, while inside her heart nearly burst. This was the man he had been and would learn to be again, the man who was confident about his body and its effect on a woman.

He pulled the shirt over his head and tossed it to her. She buried her nose in the soft material and inhaled his scent as she peered at him coyly. He was a beautifully athletic man, and the scars were only marks of honor, the same as any knight would bear if he had fought dragons.

Abruptly he turned and flipped down one side of his pants, exposing a tight haunch covered in white briefs. "I forgot my G-string," he told her solemnly.

"You'll have to pay the penalty, then. Go naked."

"Hmmm. You'd better tip big for this performance."

Sara fumbled with the tie on her robe, finally unfastening it so that the robe remained closed only by sheer luck. "I have your reward ready."

He stood very still and scrutinized her gently. "Are you blushing?"

She nodded. "We scientists are allowed to be a little shy. It's part of our image." She cleared her throat. "Go on with your show."

He pulled his pants down, bending gracefully from the waist, giving her a breathtaking view of his lean, long-legged body. The briefs remained, outlining every curve and bulge of an aroused male.

Sara's thighs relaxed as heat wound through the center of her stomach. She breathed with soft, shallow puffs, and her fair skin tingled. She knew that a mirror would have revealed that her face and chest were flushed with a fine pink mist of desire.

"Let me help with the rest," she whispered.

He moved to the edge of the bed and stood quietly, though his chest rose and fell as swiftly as hers. Sara nuzzled her face into the springy blond hair on his stomach and completed his performance with hands that trembled as they pushed his briefs down.

She moved her head lower and touched her lips to him. His hands sank into her hair convulsively. "Magnificent," she said.

He lifted her to her knees and cupped her chin in one hand. She looked up at him as her fingertips skimmed over his thighs and arousal. He traced her lips with his thumb, and devotion brimmed in his eyes. He mouthed the words *I love you.* Sara turned her face toward his palm and whispered them against the warm, callused skin.

She lay back on the bed as he knelt beside her. His hands parted her robe an inch at a time, savoring every moment. When she was bared, he let his gaze move over her just as slowly as his hands had, and the fierce love in his eyes coupled with primal need.

The moments that followed left Sara in a daze of wonder. He cared for her with his hands and his mouth, absorbed the essence of her skin and her mysteries, touched her everywhere, and brought her to an edge that made her cry out with happiness. In the midst of that pleasure he lowered himself on top of her and sighed hoarsely when she circled him with her legs.

They shared the joining, coming together on some silent signal, then following the rhythms of desire while their lips whispered words of praise and adoration. In the blue heaven of his eyes she saw a shattering that matched her own. Together, safe inside her magic and his enchantment, they made the world right again.

Nine

"Next we go out into the real world," he said as his fingertip traced a streak of afternoon sunshine across her stomach.

Sara raised her head from a rumpled pillow, lovingly eyed the chaos of her bedcovers, the empty Coco-Moo bottle that had gotten lost in them sometime during the night, and finally the naked man sprawled half on top of her with his head on her breasts.

"I don't think we're ready," she protested dryly.

"Obviously, we'd have to get dressed first."

"Yes." Smiling, she played with his golden hair, spearing her fingers through it, separating the copper strands that gave it such warm, dark undertones. "I've forgotten how to tie my shoes."

"No way, Tinker Bell. I've kept you in bed for only three days."

"But I haven't paid attention to my feet once in that whole time."

"They got you back and forth to the nursery and the kitchen."

"No, I was floating. I'm sure of it. You have that effect on me, Mr. Surprise. It's like nothing I've ever experienced before."

She felt him smile against her breast. He lapped his tongue across one of her nipples. "What flattery."

"My gorgeous man." She ran her hand down his back, lazily scratching a spot between his shoulder blades. "I know how to keep you from getting out of bed."

He made a gruff sound full of pleasure. "You think I'm helpless just because I go limp when you scratch my back."

Her laugh was throaty and confident, the sound of a woman who had been well loved. "Limp? Only on rare occasions when you're asleep."

"You've been peeking!"

From the nursery came Noelle's sleepy chatter, then the sound of the crib bumping the wall as she bounced around. Sara stretched and patted Kyle's shoulder, letting her hand linger on corded muscle and smooth, lightly freckled skin. "Baby time."

"I'll go get her."

He placed several jaunty kisses on Sara's breasts and another on her mouth before he rose from the bed. She sighed happily as she watched him pull on his T-shirt and a pair of sweat pants. He winked at her as he left the room.

She hummed with satisfaction as she put on her long blue robe and straightened the bed. After a second she heard Kyle call, "We've got a soggy-bottomed elf princess in here."

"Hold the fort. I'll be there in a second."

"Let me have a try at it. I've been the sorcerer's apprentice two or three times. Looks easy. I bet I can manage alone."

"I'll take that bet." Grinning mischievously, Sara sat down on the foot of the bed and waited. She heard Noelle giggling and Kyle talking in a low tone, the emphasized words occasionally making his progress clear.

"Ugh," she heard him say. Then, "Chew . . . toes . . . incredible contortionist . . . be still . . . wrestling . . . strong . . . ouch . . . a tornado with legs!"

"Need some help?" Sara called, trying not to laugh.

"No. I'm going to put her on the floor. I just need a bigger arena." Then, a minute later, "Run for your life! She's loose!"

Sara got up and went to the door. Noelle was crawling down the hallway, chortling at her freedom, her fresh diaper flopping open on one side, only half pinned. Kyle and Daisy followed her. Kyle wiped imaginary sweat from his forehead. "That's all I could manage before she got away." He pointed to the diaper. "It's a new style."

He swooped his hands under Noelle and picked her up. She squealed with joy and patted his face. His smile grew wide under her exploring fingers. "Who loves ya, elf princess?"

"Cal!" she squealed.

"That's right. Cal."

Sara came to the two of them, grinning, her eyes damp from the sight of trusting baby and loving man. *This* was her revenge against Valdivia.

Kyle glanced at her carefully as he stopped his sports car beside the ever-watchful dragons at the gate. Sara sat stiffly in the car's bucket seat, both arms wrapped around Noelle as if evil wizards might try to pull her away at any second.

"We're just going to lunch," Kyle reminded her.

She nodded finally. He helped her put Noelle into the baby carrier that was anchored to the backseat. When they were done, Sara faced forward and clasped her hands in her lap. Her face was pale. "I'll be fine. You just have to remember that I've geared all my energies to keeping her a secret for almost a year and a half, ever since I learned that I was pregnant. It's not easy to relax."

"You've got to believe that no one is interested in you anymore. You're just an average citizen."

"Kyle, you're the one who told me that the people from your old organization are probably keeping tabs on me. What are they going to think when they find out I have a baby?"

He chuckled. "When I said they were keeping tabs on you, I didn't mean that they're watching every move you make. They're undoubtedly curious about your research, that's all, and they'll do their best to find out what you're doing before anyone else does. But they don't care about your personal life. You're allowed to have a baby."

"But the father was . . . was Suradoran. You don't think anyone would find that disturbing? Questionable?"

Kyle reached over and brushed his fingers across her cheek. "What would our government accuse you of, Sara? Being human? Needing to take comfort from a rebel soldier? Sara, we support the rebels' cause. You didn't exactly cavort with the enemy."

"I didn't *cavort* at all," she said defensively, stiffening in the odd way she always did whenever he mentioned Noelle's father. "It wasn't, uhmmm, something I did for fun." She glanced back at Noelle, who looked a little perturbed by the emotions that were swirling around her. "But I don't regret the outcome."

"Neither do I," he said quickly. "I don't live in the past. All I care about is today, this moment. All I care about is the fact that we're together, the three of us."

She grabbed his hand and kissed it. "That's all that's important. I love you. Noelle loves you. Don't ever forget that."

Her fervor puzzled him. It was as if she were afraid of something, something she wouldn't mention. Kyle shook his worries away and decided that they were the result of being so close to her in spirit and dreams. For the first time in his life he wanted to be part of another person's future.

"We'll have to buy a stroller for Noelle," he said, smiling. "Because we'll be going out a lot, the three of us."

"Yes. *Yes.*" She sounded pleased. "The three of us."

The little town near the national park was a model of laid-back southern style. Nothing new had been built in the last forty years, but the old stores were kindly cared for and the town square was a hospitable place of giant oak trees cloaked in red fall leaves.

Kyle swung the sports car into a parking place in front of a small, homey restaurant with rocking chairs on its narrow porch. Inside they found a table in one corner and put Noelle in a high chair provided by a plump waitress who stared at the three of them without hesitation.

Kyle knew that they made an intriguing family—him with his scars and Noelle with her chocolate-colored hair and dark eyes, a coloring that a blond father and redheaded mother rarely produce. He grinned to himself. *Family.* He didn't care if anyone stared. They couldn't hurt Sara or Noelle, and the scrutiny they gave his ravaged face didn't bother him as it would have just a few weeks before. He was loved and needed; the world was perfect.

Tom and Lucy Wayne shuffled in halfway through the meal. With his buck-toothed, gold-plated grin and her pathetic shyness they looked like some insulting Hollywood version of hillbillies. They gaped like stunned trout when they spotted Sara with a baby they'd never seen before.

"What you got there, Miz Sara?" Tom asked, stomping over to their table. Lucy crept along behind him, peering over his shoulder.

Kyle glanced at Sara. Her eyes were suddenly shuttered with uncertainty. "I'm adopting a child," she said. "She's from South America."

Kyle groaned with dismay at her deception. What would it take to convince her that the past couldn't hurt her or Noelle?

"Sh-she sure is p-pretty," Lucy Wayne stuttered, nodding so vigorously that strands of her long white-blond hair shook free of its braid. "When'd you get her?"

"Just a few days ago," Sara told them.

"What place is she from?" Tom asked.

"Brazil."

He gave her a blank look, obviously not certain what Brazil was other than a type of nut. Lucy edged up to the table and stared at Noelle in awe. "You sh-shoulda t-told us. We l-love b-babies."

"Until recently I wasn't sure that the adoption would go through." Sara twisted in her seat and fumbled with Noelle's bib. Noelle seemed fascinated with Tom and Lucy. She smeared mashed potatoes everywhere but on her mouth and started to chew. Sara laughed nervously and rose from the table. "I need to clean her up." She took Noelle from the high chair and held her close. "I'll just take her to the bathroom and be right back."

"We sure look forward to seein' more of her next time we come to your place," Tom said, his eyes never leaving the baby.

"Of course. Next week. You can visit with her."

Sara hurriedly carried the baby through a set of swinging doors at the back of the restaurant. Kyle stirred restlessly, hating the discomfort this first outing had caused her and hoping that she'd stop worrying so much.

"You p-plan on stayin' at Moonspell Keep f-for a while?" Lucy inquired.

"A while."

Tom's angular face registered awe. "You must be a rich feller. You're takin' a long vacation from your job. You helpin' Miz Sara with her work?"

Tom and Lucy's questions were beginning to strike an odd chord in Kyle's mind. Suddenly alert, he gazed into Tom's carefully shuttered eyes and wondered what they hid. At the same time, Kyle grimaced at his cynical suspicions. Perhaps he'd let Sara's nervousness get to him. He gave the couple a trademark Surprise smile. It revealed nothing but good humor. "I'm just a friend of Sara's—just helping her with the new baby."

Tom studied him intently. "Well, we look forward to seein' more of you."

Kyle nodded pleasantly, wishing like hell that they'd go away. Lucy craned her head around her husband's shoulder. "Sure do want to see more of you and that baby. But for now we best be goin'."

"Didn't you come in to eat?"

"Changed our minds," Tom told him.

Lucy grinned. "You tell Sara we said good-bye."

She had lost her stutter. A warning, almost like a premonition, began to hammer inside Kyle's head. "I will."

They turned to leave. Casually Tom looked back. "Oh. Audubon says hello."

"Yes," Lucy added. "He hopes that you'll come to visit soon. Very soon."

Shock made a great stillness grow inside Kyle as he watched them leave the restaurant. Now he knew why his instincts had told him from the first that something wasn't quite right about Tom and Lucy Wayne; they were too odd. They were fakes.

Suddenly all his reassurances to Sara seemed foolish. Something was going on that he didn't understand. He could either tell her what had just happened and destroy her fragile confidence, or he could keep quiet until he knew more.

She came back from the rest room, toting a cleaned-up Noelle, who reached out to him with both arms. "She missed you," Sara said, smiling. Kyle made a great show of talking to the baby, while he silently began making plans. Audubon undoubtedly wanted to know whatever he knew about Sara, and that information must be more important than Kyle had ever imagined. Noelle's appearance was some kind of turning point. Why?

"Where are Tom and Lucy?" Sara asked, settling into a chair beside him.

"They changed their minds about eating."

She sighed with relief. "Good. Their questions made me squirm. I'm sorry about the adoption story. I just can't get over the feeling that the less anyone knows about Noelle, the better." She shook her head and looked at him with green eyes full of apology. "Do you think I'm hopelessly silly?"

Kyle grabbed her hand and brought it to his lips. "Not at all," he said.

Kyle had been quiet since their lunch at the restaurant, and Sara began to worry about his unusual brooding. She told herself that he was just exhausted—after all, she'd hardly given the poor man much chance to rest over the past few days, and she was tired too. They curled up on her queen-size bed with Noelle between them and napped all afternoon, but when Sara woke up she found Kyle standing at her bedroom window, gazing into the autumn dusk, lost in thought.

He wasn't interested in fixing supper; for the first time he let her cook. She made her gourmet specialty— hot dogs and canned soup. Afterward they sat in front of the fireplace and took turns reading an old *National Geographic* to Noelle, who snuggled next to Daisy on the rug. Noelle fell asleep in the middle of "Great Whales of the Pacific," with her head on Daisy's golden side.

"I need to make a business call to Jeopard," Kyle said. "Would you mind if I use the phone in the kitchen?

I need to sit at the kitchen table, where I can take notes."

Sara hid a feeling of dismay. He seemed secretive, and that wasn't typical of him. But she shrugged casually. "Sure. I'll put Noelle to bed and go get a couple of orchid blossoms from the greenhouse." Every night she put the orchid and milk blend on his scars. So far it had produced no effect; Sara told him to be patient, though her own results with the mixture had begun to show up more quickly.

"I won't be long," he promised, and headed for the kitchen.

Sara gave him his privacy, taking longer than necessary to get Noelle and Daisy settled in the nursery, then dawdling in the greenhouse. By the time she returned to the great room he was standing in front of the fireplace, his hands shoved into the pockets of faded jeans, his shoulders hunched under a white sweater, as if he were cold.

"Is everything okay?" she asked, going to him and slipping one arm around his waist.

He studied her so intensely that she shivered inside. "When I look at you, everything's fantastic," he said vaguely. He pulled her close. "Yes."

"You're crushing my orchids," Sara protested, chuckling. She held them up. "Ready for another treatment?"

"Ready for anything, if you're involved." He kissed her with an intensity that bordered on desperation, and his sweet wildness ignited the heat that always simmered between them.

When he stopped she looked at him groggily, her mouth feeling deliciously hot and swollen, her body flushed with expectation. "We better take care of the orchid treatment first," she whispered. "Otherwise I'm sure we'll forget."

He tilted his head toward the hearth rug. "Here, as usual?"

"Yes."

She hurried to the kitchen and blended the concoction. He had removed his sweater by the time she returned. Standing very still in front of the firelight, he was backlit in a way that made her think of an exquisite statue—a visual feast designed to arouse women during some primitive dance of fertility. Without a word he sat down on the rug; she knelt, facing him, and set the bowl of liquid to one side.

Sara dipped her fingers into the mixture and gently touched his face, stroking the worry lines on his brow as well as the scars. He sat silently, his blue eyes watching her the whole time that she smoothed her hands over his face and torso.

Sara reveled in the restrained passion they shared. She leaned forward and brushed her lips across his, then moved around behind him. His back muscles flexed and relaxed under her fingers, and she remembered how they had flexed at other times, when his whole body was moving and her hands were urging the motion.

Sara finished rubbing the orchid bath into his scars. Slowly she trailed her fingertips down his spine and languidly drew circles in the small of his back. "Done," she whispered. "Just sit still and let it dry for a minute."

He laughed hoarsely. "You touch me until all I can think about is making love to you, and then you tell me not to move. This is torture."

She knelt beside him and deftly unfastened his jeans. The breath shuddered in his throat as she uncovered him. "I'll try to make your torture easier to bear," Sara murmured, and began by kissing the hot, smooth skin low on his belly.

"Sara," he said, filling her name with a shivering mixture of encouragement and control. Then, less than a minute later, "I can't take any more, sweetheart. Come here."

There was an anguished, starving sound in his voice that made her ache to soothe him, to sweetly fill him with love. Sara took his hands. "Come with me."

She led him to her suite and they undressed each other quickly. Once they were in the shower Sara caressed and held him while the warm water cascaded over them. She trembled at the raw need in his body and was caught in his strange torment.

He jerked her close under the spray, his hands parting her, sliding wet into her most feminine secrets, building her pleasure to such a fever that she sagged against him and held tightly to his shoulders.

"Believe, believe," he said against her mouth, before his tongue swept inside to command her.

"Whatever you want. I do believe you." She answered his anguish, not the puzzling words.

Kyle grasped the backs of her thighs and lifted her against his fiercely aroused body. Then he pressed her to the tiled wall and entered her in such a slow, wickedly gyrating way that she was pulsing inside before he had hardly begun to love her. The hot water coursed down their bodies, making her nipples slide through the patterns of his chest hair, being tickled and scrubbed.

Sara gasped and cried out, and as water skimmed her lips he sank his tongue inside again. She wrapped her arms around his neck and gloried in the powerful arching of his body, the fierce possession of his hands holding her legs around his hips, the tender care he gave her with his mouth.

But as he called her name she sensed again that urgency, the melancholy that she'd never heard before. Frightened, Sara held him tightly as his warmth filled her. He trembled violently with release and continued to hold her hard against the shower wall.

"What's wrong?" she begged.

"Shh." Gradually he set her down, feathering kisses across her face as he did. Sara flicked the shower controls, and the water stopped, leaving a silence punctuated by the savage rasps of her and Kyle's breath. She gazed up at him anxiously.

"Whatever it is, tell me. Are you . . . you aren't having second thoughts about us, are you? Just say so."

He cupped her face in both hands. "Sara, no, no. My God, how could you think that?"

"You've closed yourself off from me. I don't know what to think. And you're upset about something."

He nodded. "We need to talk." He glanced down at their flushed, naked bodies. "With fewer distractions." He didn't say anything else while they dried each other off and slipped into their robes. Then he swept her into his arms and carried her to bed, where he sat down, cross-legged, in the intimate circle of light from the small lamp on her nightstand. He held her on his lap and looked down at her with troubled eyes.

"I have to leave tomorrow, on business," he told her. "I shouldn't be gone for more than two or three days."

Sara gazed at him in amazement. "Is *that* all that's worrying you? Of course, I wish you didn't have to go, but—"

"I want you to know about my work." He paused, frowning. "For years I had to be so damned expert at telling lies, or half lies, or simply misleading people by leaving out considerable portions of the truth. Audubon encouraged his agents to have a certain dramatic flair. In other words, coming up with good disguises and good con jobs was part of my job."

She felt the blood leaving her face. "Since then you've been pretty bored running an import-export business, I suppose. I've been wondering how you could be happy in an ordinary business. But what—"

"Shh. I'm getting to the *what*," he told her. "Deception made my work so much easier. But then, somewhere along the way, I realized that it had taken over more than just my work. That's what happened to

Jeopard too. He created a character that had very little humanity. It scared the hell out of the people he had to deal with, which was exactly what he wanted it to do. But eventually he *became* that character. Thank God, now he's fallen in love with a woman who sees the man he used to be. He's going to get married, maybe even have children. I don't know if she can change him completely, but she's made a good start."

"Have you lied to me about something?" Sara asked, her throat tight. "Is that what you're saying?"

He nodded. "And you don't know how much I regret the lie." He grasped her hand. "Jeopard and I don't have an import-export business down in Ft. Lauderdale. I guess you'd call us private investigators."

"You *guess*? What kind of cases do you take?"

"Hmmm. Jeopard's fiancée, Tess Gallatin, was one of our cases. You remember what I told you about her—that she's a princess?"

Sara nodded blankly. "Cherokee Indian on her father's side, and her mother was the queen of Kara. Scandinavian. How could I forget a strange story like that?"

"Tess didn't know that she had a royal background. She didn't know who her real mother was until Jeopard and I investigated her case. Actually, we were hired by someone in Kara to find out if Tess was hiding a rare blue diamond that had been stolen from the queen. Jeopard was supposed to get close to her and determine whether or not she had the diamond."

"And obviously he did."

"Yeah. But she was no thief. The diamond was a legacy from the mother she'd never met. We helped her discover her background and claim her title as a princess."

Sara held his gaze angrily. "That sounds like honorable work. Why didn't you just tell me the truth about it?"

"Because I thought you'd trust me less if you knew that I was an investigator. That you'd think that I still had ties to Audubon's group—that he'd sent me to check up on you."

Sara couldn't deny his intuition. "You were right," she muttered. Then she searched his eyes and asked bluntly, "*Do* you still have ties to the group?"

Tension filled the silence. His gaze became hard, as if he were steeling himself for her reaction. "Yes." When she stiffened he put both arms around her, the embrace like a capture. He was astute, Sara thought, because at the moment she felt like moving away from him.

"What kind of ties?" she asked coolly.

"You don't just walk away from a career with Audubon. If one of your old cases is reopened, you can be called back to duty, at least temporarily. And that's what happened to me. I have to go to Virginia to meet with Audubon."

She hugged herself and tried to fight the knot of dread growing in her stomach. "Is it about me?"

"Yes."

Sara made a soft sound of horror and covered her face. He whispered her name sadly and tried to pull her head to his shoulder, but she began to struggle, furious. "You invaded my home and now you're going to inform on me!"

"There's nothing to tell about you! Don't you understand?" He grabbed her shoulders and shook her gently. "Audubon has found out that I'm with you, and he just wants to know why—and what I've learned. All I'm going to tell him is the truth, that you're studying the medicinal uses of exotic plants."

"And that I have a baby daughter who was conceived in Surador!"

"Yes. I've told you already, no one is interested in Noelle!"

"Will you tell Audubon that you and I are lovers?"

"Yes."

Stunned, she stared at him. Then, between gritted teeth, she whispered, "Be sure to describe the details. How I moved, how my body felt, what I said in your ear—"

"Stop it!" His eyes glittered with torment that matched her own. "Sure, I'll tell him that we're lovers. I'll tell him that we *love* each other. I'll tell him that I want to marry you and be a father to your daughter, and that all the three of us want is to be left alone!"

"The government will never leave me alone! They want something from me!"

"We're not talking about the government, Sara. We're talking about Audubon. He's free-lance. Don't be stubborn and foolish. You've got nothing to be afraid of. Not Audubon. Not me."

"You planned to get information on me right from the first."

"No. I came here as a friend, I swear. Hell, Sara, I came here because I couldn't get you out of my mind. I had to prove to myself that I ought to forget you, because you'd never want to get involved with me and my scars. I thought that once I knew that there was no hope, I could go on with my life. Thank God, I was wrong—you need me as much as I need you. I won't let anything ruin things for us now."

She glared at him through tear-filled eyes. "If your brother adopted a professional persona that was cold and cruel, what persona did you take?"

His jaw flexed; he eyed her with both despair and frustration. "I'm trying to be as honest with you as I can. I'll tell you more as time goes on. You can trust me."

"I don't even know you." She braced her hands against his chest and tried to push herself away. For a second his grip tightened on her arms, but when she began to struggle he let her go. She scooted away and crouched on the foot of the bed, feeling like an animal protecting its den.

"I think I understand your disguise," she said, her voice low and broken. "Jeopard tricks people by making them fear him; you trick people by making them trust you."

He inhaled softly. "Yes. I'm good at it too. When it's necessary, I can make friends with the deadliest S.O.B.s you've ever imagined. Then I use that friendship to put them away, to keep them from hurting innocent people. I'm a little ashamed of how good I am at the con jobs, but I'm not ashamed of what I've accomplished because of it. *I've never tried to con the people I love.*"

"Don't go see Audubon. Tell him to take a flying leap."

"I can't, Sara. Despite what you think, his motivations are good. Inside your mind you're carrying the know-how to create a herbicide so powerful that a teaspoonful would wipe out most of the greenery in this state. It's his job to keep track of you. And when one of his former agents is living with you, it's his job to ask for an explanation. Look, why would I tell you all of this if it weren't true? Why would I risk your distrust?"

"Because you're worried that I'd find out the truth about you anyway."

His shoulders slumped. "How much do you really want to trust me? There's something inside you that I don't understand, something that you seem to be holding back. I think this is a good excuse for you to put me at arm's length because you're hiding something else."

She trembled violently. She'd thought that she and Noelle were so safe. Sara reminded herself that Kyle hadn't deceived her more than she was still deceiving him. *But you're doing it for his own good. Think how the truth would hurt not only Noelle, but him.* Sara turned away from him and huddled on the end of the bed, staring fixedly at the floor. "You'll be leaving for Virginia in the morning, to see Audubon?"

"Yes. Sara, I—"

"I think you ought to sleep in the guest room tonight."

His voice came back graveled with anger and sorrow. "I don't want to leave you alone with your morbid fears and suspicions."

"When you're gone I won't have anything to fear." The obscenity that came from his mouth had a wounded sound that tore at her. "There's one other thing to consider," she said desperately. "If you leave the keep, I'll make certain that you never get back in. So, don't leave."

She heard him stand up. Slowly she turned her head to look at him. His eyes were cold, his face an angry mask made cruel by the scars. "I'll get back in," he told her. "Count on it." He let his gaze flicker over her for a second. "I'll get back in."

He left the room, closing the door behind him with a slow, confident motion of his hand, and she felt as if he had just made her his prisoner.

Ten

Confused and exhausted from a sleepless night, Sara dressed in a sweater and pink overalls, combed her hair neatly, and hid her emotions. She waited for Kyle in the kitchen at dawn, with a pot of coffee made. He walked in brusquely, dropped his big leather tote bag on the floor, gazed at her with troubled, searching eyes, and then said, "Well?" as if he were expecting her judgment, guilty or innocent.

"I keep thinking that Noelle trusted you at first sight."

"And?"

"Maybe I should have faith in her opinion. I don't know."

Sara noted that his eyes were ringed with shadows and he had nicked his chin shaving. His golden hair was rumpled. His jogging shoes were sloppily laced. He'd already put on his blue down jacket over his jeans and white sweater, and the jacket collar was haphazardly turned under on one side.

He didn't look like a sophisticated, conniving super-agent. He looked very human and very much in need of a hug. She groaned inwardly with frustration. Perhaps it was an act. Perhaps. No. She couldn't tell. Yes. Maybe.

Finally, her head felt as if it would burst with indecision. All she could do was stare at his jacket and luggage with a sinking heart. "You're leaving right now?"

"The sooner I go, the sooner I'll get it over with, the sooner I can come back here and try to convince you that I'm not your enemy."

"All right." From the kitchen table she got a plastic bag filled with orchid blossoms. "Would you like them? There's enough for two days. You really shouldn't miss a day using them. Even if you don't have a blender you can crush them up in a glass of milk."

A muscle flexed in his jaw. His eyes softened, but only a little. "Thank you." She handed him the bag and stepped back. He laid it carefully on his tote.

"Would you like a cup of coffee before you go?"

"No."

"I know that my coffee tastes a little like a bad lab experiment, but—"

"I don't think we'll solve anything by drawing out the good-byes, Sara. Do you trust me any more than you did last night?"

Wretched, she looked at him. "I honestly don't know. I don't know what to believe."

"Honest." He made the word sound unsavory.

"Would you like to say good-bye to Noelle?"

"I already have. She was asleep. I even told Daisy good-bye." He grunted with dismay and almost sounded amused. "I don't think Daisy heard me. She was snoring too loud."

Sara stuck her hands in her side pockets and clenched them. "So you're all set. I'll walk you to the door."

"You'd better ride down to the gate with me." He dug the remote control from a jacket pocket. "Don't you want this back? Don't want me to have easy access, do you?"

"Why not? Do you enjoy using your Tarzan act to get over the garden walls? I thought I'd let you use the gate next time."

"I wanted to give you a sporting chance to make good on your threat to keep me out."

She laughed dully. "In a calmer moment I realized how ridiculous my threat was. I might as well try to keep crab grass out of a garden."

"My root takes that as a compliment."

Sara shrugged. "I like crab grass."

He slipped the remote control back into his pocket, took the bag of delicate orchid blossoms in one hand, and picked up his tote with the other. Sara followed him from the kitchen. *He's going to visit a man who's a stranger to me, and he's going to tell that man the personal information about my life.*

By the time they reached the entrance foyer her teeth were gritted and her resolve solid. Sara took the ornate key ring from the antelope horn and unlocked the door. She could feel Kyle's gaze on her face every second of the time, and she steadfastly ignored him. But her hands fumbled with the electronic lock, and she needed three tries to get the code right. "Damn."

"Which did you forget—your IQ or your birth date?"

"My reason for letting you know this code in the first place." She pulled the door open and stood beside it like an usher.

With one of his easy, loping strides he moved close to her. In another instant his lips brushed a gentle good-bye across her forehead. She shut her eyes to squeeze back tears.

"Keep the dragons at bay until I come back to help you fight them," he said.

When she opened her eyes to let the obstinate tears flow freely, he was gone.

Audubon's home had become extremely familiar to Kyle over the years. It served very tastefully as the group's headquarters, and when Audubon called an agent in for a meeting, that agent was treated with all the polite hospitality of a master host, which Audubon was.

Kyle gazed out the window of his suite at white fences and sprawling pastures stocked with polo ponies. Like everything in Audubon's fashionable, old-money world, they were carefully chosen for quality and variety, like the selections in Audubon's wine cellars, the classic cars in his garage, and the glamorous women who paraded through Audubon's life.

From somewhere downstairs in the mansion a gong began to sound, as if heralding the arrival of royalty. Dimly Kyle heard a helicopter approaching the estate. He glanced out the window and spotted it, a large custom model, one of Audubon's favorite toys. The gong kept pounding. Audubon loved grand gestures and melodrama. If he ever saw Sara's castle, he would probably want to buy it.

Within a few minutes one of Audubon's assistants called on the suite's phone and told Kyle that Audubon was home and waiting to see him in the study. Kyle went downstairs and followed a large hallway to a room where elegance was embodied in English antiques, classic paintings, sterling silver polo trophies, and mahogany bookcases crammed with a fortune in rare editions.

In the center of it all was Audubon with his combat boots propped on the corner of a massive antique desk. His jungle fatigues were wrinkled and sweat-stained; one hand was bandaged around the palm, and a tiny spot of blood had already soaked through the gauze.

But Audubon's flowing snow-white hair—his one true vanity, he claimed—was impeccably styled, and Kyle took that as a sign that the mission, whatever it had been, had gone well.

"Long trip?" he asked, reaching across the desk to shake Audubon's good hand.

"To hell and back." Audubon rarely smiled, but satisfaction was tucked into the squint lines around his dark eyes. "I had to make a quick little jaunt out of the country. Sorry to keep you waiting. I get the idea that you're not feeling very patient right now."

Kyle lowered himself into a leather armchair across from the desk. "No. I want to know the story on Dr. Scarborough."

"So would I, if I were you."

"Why have you had two agents watching her all this time?"

"How do you like their Ma and Pa Kettle act?"

"Not bad. They won her mother's trust, and when Sara came home from Surador, Anna assured her that good ol' Tom and Lucy Wayne were trustworthy. Perfect. Congratulations. But why is that kind of surveillance necessary?"

Audubon tilted his majestic head in acknowledgment of Kyle's grim tone. "Hmmm. You're not interested just for professional reasons."

"That's right." Quickly, and with very few details, he explained what had happened between him and Sara. "She's scared," he told Audubon. "And I keep telling her that she has no reason to be. Should I be worried that I'm misleading her?"

Audubon steepled his fingers against his mouth and looked at Kyle somberly. "The herbicide she created was a hoax."

"A hoax?"

"It doesn't hold up under testing. The compound is no doubt deadly, but when it's exposed to air for more than a few seconds, it becomes harmless. In other words, the herbicide is a winner in the lab and a loser in the real world."

"There was no way she could have known that when she created it for Valdivia. He was so impatient that he didn't give her time to do any tests outside the lab."

"So she told us."

"Why would she lie about it?"

"Maybe she didn't. Maybe she had no idea that her experiment was a failure. It's difficult to know what to believe about her motives. That's why we've been keeping track of her all this time. Waiting for something to give us a clue to the truth."

"She's got nothing to hide. She hated being forced to concoct the damned herbicide for Valdivia, and I can't blame her. It wouldn't shock me if she had deliberately tried to sabotage it. But I don't think she knows whether she did or not. Why don't the government boys just politely ask her? It's not a question she'd shy away from answering."

Audubon probed him with dark, sharp eyes. "What did she tell you about her child?"

"The father was a soldier. Must have been one of Miguel Santos's men, since I understand that they were the ones who helped with the escape. She was in shock. She needed a friend. He was in the right place at the right time. The baby was born nine months after she came home."

"And you have no reason to doubt that story?"

"No." Kyle held the stern gaze across the desk from him, silently warning Audubon not to let professional cynicism mock Sara's integrity. "She's one of the ones you've always talked about. One of the ones who makes everything worth the effort."

"I want her to be worth it. Believe me. You know better than to think I want anything less."

"Then what are you trying to tell me?"

Suddenly Audubon looked tired, a rare and disturbing thing for him. He drew his feet down and leaned forward on the desk. His eyes were hard, but not cruel. They seemed to scan Kyle's scars for a moment. "Before the kidnapping—if it *was* a kidnapping—she was Valdivia's mistress. And we're fairly certain that her child is Valdivia's daughter."

•   •   •

Sara made her decision and called Tom Wayne. She asked if he wanted some geese, free of charge. "They'll be hell to round up," she warned.

"Oh, I'll be glad to come get 'em!" he said, sounding very enthusiastic, which puzzled her a little. "Me and Lucy been talkin' about that little girl of yours. We sure would like to see her again."

Sara rubbed her head distractedly. She was trying to give Kyle the benefit of the doubt. She had been foolish and stubborn. She shouldn't live in fear anymore, not because of her past, or Kyle's questions, or Audubon's surveillance. She shouldn't rely on protection from a flock of maniacal geese. And she shouldn't worry about a couple of harmless people who loved babies and simply wanted to visit with Noelle.

"Sure," she told Tom. "Why don't you and Lucy come over tomorrow? You can visit with the baby and I'll tell you all about her."

"All about her?" Tom echoed. "That's just what we'd hoped for, Miz Sara. Just what we'd hoped for."

The next day Tom loaded the geese into his van with Sara's help. She lured them with an offer of crushed corn. Afterward she and Tom walked back into the castle and sat down on the hearth rug, where Lucy was stretched out with Noelle bouncing on her back. Daisy stood close by, looking a little perturbed by the stranger who was playing with her baby.

"Sh-she really is a w-wonder," Lucy said, pushing her thick glasses up a little. "Do you have any p-pictures of h-her when she w-was newborned?"

Sara smiled. "Yes."

Tom looked at her quizzically. "But you said you just got her."

Sara winced at her carelessness. "The adoption agency sent a few photographs. I'll see if I can find them. Be right back."

She went to her bedroom and rummaged around in a dresser drawer filled with instant snapshots, the kind that develop themselves while the photographer watches. Sara chose several close-ups of Noelle. It would be impossible for Tom or Lucy to tell where they had been taken. Pleased with her progress, however small, toward becoming more open and trusting, she walked back into the great room with the snapshots held up proudly. "Here you—"

She stopped, speechless at the sight of Lucy sitting alone on the couch, her glasses gone, her expression somehow more sophisticated than before. "Where are Tom and Noelle?" Sara asked, trying not to sound anxious.

Lucy Wayne—stuttering, pathologically shy Lucy—looked at her calmly and said, "Dr. Scarborough, there's no need to be alarmed, I assure you."

Sara was dimly aware of the snapshots fluttering from her hand. "Who are you?"

"We work for Audubon."

Horror clawed at Sara's throat. "Where is my baby?"

"My partner has left with her. Daisy went along too."

White-hot fury poured into Sara's fear. She had never been a violent person, but the idea that these people had schemed to steal her daughter drove everything but maternal fury from her mind.

She grabbed a poker from the hearth and advanced on the tall blond woman, who stood swiftly and held up both hands in a placating gesture. "All you and I have to do is follow them, Dr. Scarborough. My partner is taking Noelle to Virginia. To Audubon. He thought this would be the simplest way to get you there without a problem."

"Have you ever heard of the Bill of Rights or the Constitution?" Sara shouted. "You people can't come into my home and take my child!"

The blond agent vaulted gracefully over the couch as

Sara advanced. Keeping the couch between the two of them, she eyed Sara's lethally raised poker with grim consternation. "You're a very intelligent, calm, logical person, Dr. Scarborough. Be reasonable."

"I'm Noelle's mother! I want my daughter back, or I'm going to very intelligently, calmly, and logically wrap this poker around your neck!"

"It's too late to change the plan. My partner's already driven off the estate with Noelle and Daisy in the van. Relax, Dr. Scarborough. My partner raised five sisters. He's terrific with children. Noelle will be just fine. You go pack some clothes, do whatever you have to do to close this place up for a couple of days, and I'll be waiting right here. We'll take your car. All Audubon wants is some answers to a few questions."

"He wants to coerce me into something I don't want to do!"

"No, he just wants the truth. Now, come on, Dr. Scarborough. Kyle Surprise is already waiting for you up in Virginia. You obviously trust him. You can trust me too."

Sara stopped by the couch, the poker raised like a baseball bat. A sudden thought made her hands quiver on the wrought iron handle. "Did Kyle know who you really are?"

"Yes. But not until a couple of days ago."

The poker wavered. Finally Sara let it sink to the floor. "Was he in on this plan to take my daughter?"

"I can't discuss these issues with you, Doctor. I don't have the clearance. You'll have to ask Kyle yourself."

Sara staggered to the fireplace and rested her head against the cool, familiar stones. Maybe Kyle had set her up. Had he planned it from the first day? She wanted to cry, but she had no tears. She had only a numb, single-minded determination to get Noelle back and then never let anyone dangerous get near her again.

• • •

Audubon's housekeeper kept coming to the door of the garden room to glance at Kyle as if wondering when he would do something appropriate, like either go into a drunken rage or curl up, pitifully, on the floor, as potted as the ficus trees.

Kyle was also aware that Audubon stopped by the door occasionally but didn't say anything. There were no worthwhile words of wisdom; no words that would carve the bitterness out of Kyle's chest, and Audubon knew that.

Kyle sat in the darkness for hours, his head resting on the smooth back grid of a wicker chair. He held an untouched bottle of bourbon and contemplated throwing it at the plants because they reminded him of Sara's greenhouse. Only last night he had crumpled two of the rare orchids she'd given him into a glass of milk and spread the strange mixture on his face and body, reveling in memories of Sara's touch. He had begun to doubt that her whimsical orchid treatment was going to help his scars, but using it made him feel closer to her.

Tonight, beyond a ceiling of shimmering glass, the night sky was mercilessly cold and overcast. Kyle wanted to merge his thoughts with that sky and forget the image that kept hammering against his skull—Sara making love to Diego de Valdivia. Whether she had plotted some kind of twisted scam with the bastard was still undetermined, though it seemed logical. How could she have been his mistress, then the victim of his kidnapping, and then become his mistress again, bearing his child, a child that she adored?

No. She must have helped him fake the kidnapping. But why? And why create a herbicide that didn't work? He shut his eyes. Unless there was another herbicide, the real one, deadly and effective, and Valdivia had sold it to the highest bidder while Audubon's people were concentrating on a fake. Somewhere along the way

Valdivia's plan had gone awry; he had ended up dead, but Sara had gone free.

The scenario was a convoluted mess; there were too many questions that only Sara could answer. But about one thing there was no doubt, and it damned every claim of innocence she might try to make: Audubon had proof of her happy, voluntary, long-term affair with Valdivia.

Kyle raised a hand to the scars on his face, and his stomach twisted with nausea. Had she shared Valdivia's bed the night after . . . he leaned forward, set the bottle of bourbon on the floor, and buried his head in his hands. Dear God, he loved her so much, and he was shriveling up inside until there was nothing left but that awful, tormenting love and so much bitterness that he didn't know which way to turn.

"Kyle?" Audubon lounged in the doorway, looking casual and yet never relaxed, his military clothes changed for loafers, dark slacks, and a gray pullover that was probably made of cashmere. "Mike Antonetti just got here. With the baby. And the dog." Audubon paused, then said, smiling, "And a lot of geese."

"What makes you think I want to see Valdivia's bastard daughter?"

Kyle hated those words, but he stood up and faced Audubon belligerently. From somewhere toward the front of the mansion he heard the soft, tired mewlings of an unhappy Noelle. The marrow seemed to flow out of his bones, and his knees went weak. "There's no reason for me to see her yet," he muttered.

"Sara Scarborough will be here soon. Are you going to be ready to talk to her?"

"I'm retired, not senile. If you need help getting answers from her, I won't screw up my part."

Audubon turned toward the sound of footsteps approaching the garden room. "Mop," a tiny voice called sadly. "Mop."

"Mop?" Audubon inquired. He flicked a wall switch and recessed fixtures filled the garden room with soft light.

Kyle squinted and rubbed his eyes, glad for an excuse to force the sting from them. "She's calling for her mother."

Mike Antonetti, alias Tom Wayne, appeared beside Audubon. With his fake buckteeth gone and his hair pulled back neatly, he was almost unrecognizable. In his arms he carried Noelle, who was wrapped in a baby blanket. Daisy shoved between his legs and came to Kyle, whining and wagging her tail as if very relieved to see him.

He stared miserably at Noelle. Her tear-swollen eyes went wide with recognition. Both little arms shot toward him. "Cal!" She wiggled in Antonetti's arms and made a tragic, pleading sound.

"Sorry about this," Audubon said, looking uncomfortable. "I had no idea." He motioned to Mike Antonetti. "Take her upstairs."

When Mike turned to leave, Noelle began to cry with tiny, gulping sobs, while she reached toward Kyle frantically. Kyle swayed in place. He felt as if invisible hands were pulling him apart inside. Daisy poked her nose into his hand and whined again.

Noelle's crying was the most heartbreaking—and broken—sound he'd ever heard in his life. "Cal. Cal," she finally managed, and slumped against Antonetti's shoulder, so exhausted that she was gasping for breath.

"Take her upstairs," Audubon said again, to Mike.

"Cal," Noelle whimpered, gazing at Kyle with bewildered, tragic eyes.

Mike started walking away. Kyle's control broke apart. "Wait." Kyle strode to him, fiercely ignored Audubon's scrutiny, and took Noelle. She wrapped both arms around his neck and kissed him several times, then burrowed her head into the crook of his shoulder like a mouse curling up for the night.

Kyle turned his back to the other men, swallowing hard to get control of the knot in his throat. "I'll hold her for a few minutes and then take her upstairs."

"This is going to be more of a problem for you than I ever expected," Audubon said quietly. "It might be best if you let me talk to Dr. Scarborough alone."

Kyle went to the chair and sat down. He realized that he was embracing Noelle so tightly that she was squirming a little. He stroked her back in apology, and she murmured happily. He swiveled to stare at Audubon. "At the moment I don't know what the hell I'm doing, but it won't have any effect on me later. Just leave me alone with the kid. It's way past her bedtime and she doesn't have her pacifier or her rubber frog. That's why she's so upset."

"Oh, I see," Audubon said dryly. "I could swear that she's perfectly content without her pacifier or rubber frog, now that she has you."

He and Antonetti left the room. Daisy collapsed by Kyle's feet, sighing heavily. Kyle shut his eyes and tried not to remember who had fathered the little angel who was snuggled deep in his arms, but he remembered her mother in excruciating detail, and bitterness left very little room for mercy.

Eleven

Kyle was waiting for her, Sara thought, sad and angry. He was waiting to help Audubon interrogate her. No matter what his motives, no matter how much he might cajole, tease, or gently prod for a truth she wouldn't give, she would never forget that he had conned her into this situation. He had helped steal her baby.

Lucy Wayne's real name was Victoria Coursey. Victoria was an ex-actress turned cop turned Audubon agent. In her purse she carried a small automatic pistol and a picture of her pet hamster. She was disgustingly calm at all times.

Which was the opposite of Sara as Victoria guided the station wagon along the driveway through Audubon's estate. In the darkness beyond acres of manicured lawns sat a Tudor-style mansion. The exterior was dramatically lit by flood lamps; the mansion was both forbidding and stately.

Sara's heart thudded, and the muscles of her back felt as if they would snap. She was frightened now . . . and furious and ready for battle. And when she let herself think about a future without Kyle she could scarcely keep herself from crying.

Victoria parked the wagon in a brick courtyard. Together she and Sara walked to an impressive entrance inset with ornately carved doors. Sara jumped when they swung open without warning. A tall, rugged man with dark eyes, dark eyebrows, and a mane of snow-white hair stood there, one hand on each door.

It was a dramatic confrontation; Sara suspected that it had been planned that way. "Dr. Scarborough, how nice of you to let us force you into coming here," he said in a deep, cultured drawl. Then he smiled pleasantly and extended a hand. "T.L.B. Audubon. Please, call me Audubon."

She ignored his hand. "I want my daughter back."

"Of course. Come inside." He angled the hand toward Victoria, who shook it quickly. "Good work."

"Dr. Scarborough made it pleasant."

"I threatened her with a fireplace poker," Sara corrected her grimly. "And I'm not too far from being violent now. *I want to see my daughter immediately.*"

"Please. Come inside. Your daughter arrived just thirty minutes ago. She's happy and comfortable, I assure you. Now, let's see what we can do about making you feel the same way."

He led them through the mansion to a large study, where a fire crackled under a marble mantelpiece crowded with gleaming trophies. "Sit down, Dr. Scarborough."

Victoria waited by the door to the study. "Do you want me to stay, Audubon?"

He waved a hand at her. "Thank you, no. Good night. I'll speak with you and Mike early in the morning."

Victoria nodded. "Good night, then. Good night, Dr. Scarborough." When Sara didn't answer, she left the room.

Sara stood firmly in the middle of the study, her hands clenched. Audubon flashed a beautiful smile. "Please, let me take your coat."

Sara shrugged her arms out of a wine-colored cloth overcoat but clutched it to her stomach defiantly. Audubon's eyes flickered with intrigue at the sight of her white sneakers, pink overalls, and the pink and white sweater underneath the overalls. The sweater had a line of unicorns across the chest. Sara glared at him coldly.

"I don't look much like someone who's sinister, do I?" she asked sarcastically. "Well, I'm not."

"Your coat, please."

"I'm not staying."

"We have a lot to discuss, Doctor."

"Not until I see my baby."

"No. We talk first." He went to a massive desk, where he sat down, and swung both loafered feet onto one corner. He pressed a button on a phone console and said simply, "Dr. Scarborough is here."

He released the button without waiting for an answer. Audubon gestured toward a plush leather armchair. "Please. It's against my nature to sit while a lady stands."

"But it's not against your nature to spy on innocent people and coerce them. Hilarious sense of priorities you've got." Sara's ears caught the distant sound of measured, forceful footsteps crossing marbled floors and growing louder with each second. Kyle? She twisted toward the study door, every nerve on alert. Just let the traitor give her one reassuring smile! Just let him try to soothe her hurt feelings!

He stepped through the doorway and halted, gazing at her with blue eyes so cold that she shivered. Sara stared at the contempt she found there, and her throat constricted with horror. *He knows about Valdivia and me.*

"Your daughter is asleep," he told her, his voice threaded with distaste, as if it took great effort for him to speak to her at all. "You can see her after you answer my questions. If you want something to drink or eat before we get started, say so right now. There's a bathroom down the hall if you want it."

"No," Sara muttered, stepping back numbly. She went to the armchair and sat down, still hugging her coat against her stomach. She was empty, beaten, ruined. No one could prove or disprove that she had been Valdivia's willing accomplice, but the accusations would destroy the secrets she had so desperately hoped to keep for Noelle's sake. And for Kyle's.

Sara gazed at him wretchedly as he went to a bookcase beside the hearth and leaned against it, his arms crossed over his chest. He had changed into dress shoes, dark trousers, and a pale blue dress shirt, open at the neck. The cuffs of the sleeves were fastened with monogrammed silver links. The silver matched that on the latches of the dark leather suspenders he wore. His hair was neatly styled in a way she'd never seen before. The man who gazed down at her with his face set in a rigid mask was not the same man who had been her friend and lover, and he wanted her to know it.

"We'll start at the beginning," he told her. "And it will be simpler if you tell the truth. When did you first meet Diego de Valdivia?"

Sara leaned back in the chair and shut her eyes. She could only hope to escape from this ordeal with a little of her dignity intact. If she thought about the loathing in Kyle's eyes, she would fall apart. If she thought about her own innocence, she would become too bitter to talk. "I met him one year before the kidnapping."

"We'll get to the so-called 'kidnapping' later. Where did you meet him?"

"In Quetano. I'd gone into the city for a short vacation, after working in the rain forest for several months. He was there on business. We met in a hotel restaurant. I was eating alone. He asked if he could join me. We had a mutual acquaintance, a professor at the local university. He was interested in my research into agricultural herbicides. We talked about his coffee bean plantations."

"When did the relationship become personal?"

Sara gazed at him. His tone of voice whipped her. In self-defense she let sorrow and frustration build a wall that allowed only the most essential details to escape. "Are you asking me—"

"How long after the first meeting in the hotel restaurant did you start sleeping with him?"

She sucked in a tight little breath. "Eventually."

Kyle's mouth formed a merciless smile. "A few months later? A few days? A few minutes after dessert? What?"

"A few months."

"You saw a lot of him before then?"

"Yes. Whenever we were both in the city."

"Let me tell you what we know, and then you think about repeating this part of your story—and give me the true version. Diego de Valdivia had a reputation with women. The kind of reputation that a bull in a barn full of eager cows might envy. He wasn't known for patience. He wasn't the type who would chase a woman for several months before he got her into bed."

"Think what you want. I told you the truth."

"So you successfully played innocent with a sadistic, amoral man who as far as we know never had a long-term relationship with a woman before. You want me to believe that?"

Sara dug her fingernails into the chair arms. "I met him, he was interested in my work; he was intelligent, charming, and very attentive. I thought he was a legitimate Suradoran businessman. He was good at hiding what he really wanted, which was to know about my work with viral herbicides. I explained that what I hoped to do was create a cheap, environmentally safe compound for agricultural use. A weed killer that wouldn't hurt anything but the weeds."

"So, what attracted you to him sexually? His fascination for farming?"

"I had a . . . a relationship with him for several months," she continued doggedly. "I thought for a very brief time that I loved him. But before long I realized that he was using me to get information. I told him so. I broke off the relationship. He made some very ugly threats, but I thought he was bluffing. He left me alone. I assumed that I wouldn't have to worry about him. I never expected that he was so determined that he'd follow when I went back to the States to visit my mother."

Audubon interjected, "Where you're saying that he kidnapped you—and Dinah McClure, a friend who happened to be with you at the time."

"Yes."

"A pretty damned weak story," Kyle told her. "So you let Valdivia haul you back to one of his plantations in Surador where he *forced* you to create the kind of herbicide he wanted, something so deadly it could be of military value. And you did what he asked without quibbling."

"I was a *prisoner*. He threatened to send people to hurt my mother. He threatened to hurt me. He even threatened to hurt Dinah, who was pregnant. He would have, too, even though he was obsessed with Dinah—he actually seemed to love her."

Kyle slashed the air with one hand. "So you ignored your romantic feelings for him? You were some sort of martyr for Dinah's sake, when your lover admitted that he loved *her*?" His voice rose. "Tell the damned truth, Dr. Scarborough. You were still sleeping with Valdivia, the kidnapping was a hoax, and Dinah McClure was the only *innocent* person in the whole deal."

Sara trembled with rage at the unfairness of her situation. She had no proof, Kyle would never believe her, no one would believe her, and nothing she could say would make any difference. "I hated him," she retorted, her voice low and fierce. "I was forced to work for him. I was glad when he died. I'm innocent. You can despise me for having been Valdivia's lover before the kidnapping, but you're wrong for thinking I collaborated with him."

"Despise you?" Kyle said softly, his eyes narrowing. "It might be different if I thought you were telling the truth."

She held his gaze levelly, cruel and unrelenting. "No. I've always known that you wouldn't want me anymore if you knew that I had been touched by the man who put those scars on you."

His eyes glittered with fury that was mixed with an anguish that made her heart ache no matter how much she tried to ignore it. "You're still telling one lie after another."

Sara laughed wearily and put her head in her hands. "What now?"

Audubon cleared his throat. "Noelle is Valdivia's daughter."

She jerked her head up instantly. "No." She would never stop protecting Noelle. She would reveal nothing, not even in self-defense, that might be repeated to Noelle someday.

"Yes," Kyle countered sharply. "You were sleeping with the bastard up until the time my brother showed up. You were lucky that you were able to pull off the innocent-victim act."

"I must be a great actress. *Diego de Valdivia is not Noelle's father.*"

"Give us the father's name, then."

She flinched. "I . . . I never learned his name."

"Convenient. You must have been hot as hell for the guy to be in too big a hurry to catch even a first name. I tell you, Doctor, I had no idea that you used so little restraint."

She was drowning in despair, and suddenly so tired that she could barely fight anymore. It was hopeless anyway. "A rebel soldier is Noelle's father—"

"Why did you fake the herbicide you gave us?" Audubon asked, his dark eyes boring into her. "And who got the real herbicide?"

"You mean it didn't hold up under further testing?"

"That's right. It's worthless as a weapon."

"Thank God!"

Kyle gave her a derisive look. "You're going to go to prison if we find out that you gave a different version of the herbicide to Valdivia's people. And if you go to prison, your daughter will probably be put up for adoption."

She stared at him in shock. His announcement almost broke her. "I didn't. I didn't." She gulped for air and said loudly, "I did *not* give anything to anybody else! I did the best I could to create a hoax that would fool Valdivia, but I didn't know if I had succeeded!" She stood, shaking badly. "You can't make charges against me, because I didn't do anything wrong. All you have is suspicion and circumstantial evidence. I want my daughter now. We're going home."

Audubon shook his head. "In the morning we'll be doing a blood test on her. You see, Valdivia had a number of children by different women. We've got blood samples from a few of them. You're a biologist—you know what kind of conclusions the new tests can give us when we compare Noelle's genetic material to that of the other children. We'll know for certain whether she's Valdivia's daughter."

Sara grasped the back of the chair and held on. Her knees threatened to buckle. "I think you're lying about the other children."

"No," Kyle told her, his tone thick and troubled, as if he'd had as much as he could take for the moment too. "But if you want to put Noelle through the pain of giving a blood sample, we'll do it. Personally, I don't like the idea of sticking her with a needle to get an answer that you could give us easily."

Sara looked from him to Audubon. "It's pointless to keep pretending," Audubon said, not unkindly.

"I . . . we don't want to draw Noelle into this," Kyle added, his voice leaden.

Sara turned furious, tear-filled eyes on him. "Don't offer your concern. She's nothing to you anymore." Tears slid down her face and she almost sagged. "To you she's just . . . Diego de Valdivia's daughter."

Kyle's expression tightened, and his eyes no longer looked cold, only sad. The scars stood out vividly, almost as if taunting her to remember that she was indirectly responsible for them. "Thank you for making this simple for all of us." He turned away and stared into the fire, his fists clenched by his sides.

"So tell us about your relationship with Valdivia," Audubon prodded. "Let's say that you did break off with him, that he did kidnap you later and hold you hostage for upwards of a year, that you were forced to work for him, and that you weren't personally plotting anything illegal with your research. How would you describe your romantic relationship with Valdivia during the time in which you were held hostage, the time when your daughter was conceived?"

Sara faced him bitterly, reckless and broken-hearted. "None of your business. I don't care what else you say or do, or what else you threaten me with. I've been humiliated enough. I wanted to protect my daughter from the past, and I failed." She glanced at Kyle, who still had his back to her. "I wanted to have a new life with a man I trusted and loved. That's lost, now, too."

She was dimly aware of Kyle pivoting to gaze at her. She couldn't bring herself to look at him. Instead, she kept her eyes riveted to Audubon's. "You can accuse me of having poor judgment about Diego de Valdivia.

That's the only thing I'm guilty of. Now let me go and try to make a life with what little peace of mind I have left."

Audubon's expression never changed. But after a moment of looking into her eyes he slowly lifted one hand and gestured toward the door. "Your daughter," he said softly, "is upstairs in the fifth bedroom on the right. You may spend the night as my guest, or you may take her and leave."

Sara looked at Kyle, then. "Is there any reason why I'll ever have to see you again?"

He seemed drained, troubled, as tormented as he was angry. "No."

"Then I hope you respect my privacy. I'm sure you agree that Noelle should be allowed to forget you as quickly as possible." Sara had to fight with her voice to keep it from revealing all her despair. It was a losing battle. "She . . . she couldn't possibly understand . . . of course."

"Sara—"

"Things are different," she said in a rush of emphasis. "You've destroyed so much . . . please don't destroy the rest."

"I understand," he said wearily.

She snatched her coat up and ran from the room.

Ft. Lauderdale. It should have felt good to be back in the sun again, good to be near the beaches and the ocean, in a pastel-hued city where the most pressing problem was how to handle the annual spring break madness. But it all seemed dark and colorless to Kyle as he left the airport in a low-slung red convertible. The weather was warm and muggy, typical for October. Before Kyle went to his brother's town house he stopped by his own place, an old beach cottage that he had restored, as he had the car he was driving. He told himself that home was where he wanted to be, and he changed into shorts and a polo shirt.

Tess Gallatin was similarly attired when she answered the bell at Jeopard's town house, though her darkly exotic beauty made even shorts and a T-shirt seem special. With one hand she was trying to fasten a long clip into her shoulder-length black hair, but when she saw Kyle's face she dropped the clip and clasped both hands to her mouth in astonishment.

"What did you do? Oh, Kyle, Kyle!" Her lilting English voice made even shock sound musical. She turned and called toward the back, "Jep! Kyle is home! Come here quickly!" Then she grasped Kyle's hands and pulled him inside a coolly elegant, white-on-white living room.

She barely had time to shut the door before Jeopard Surprise came striding into the room, a long white robe belted around his waist, his light blond hair still wet from a shower. He stopped abruptly and stared at Kyle as Tess had done.

"When did this happen?" he asked.

Kyle sat down on a sofa and rubbed his face wearily. He was more distraught over it than happy, at least at the moment. "It was this way when I got up this morning." To say it had been that way when he *woke* up would have been inaccurate, since he hadn't slept last night after Sara's departure from the mansion.

"You want to explain?" Jeopard prodded. He and Tess sat down on a facing sofa.

"I've been using a concoction that Sara Scarborough fixed for me. Something she made up from rare plants in her greenhouse. Until this morning I hadn't seen any results."

"The scars look so much lighter," Tess said in an awed tone. "It's a vast difference. Will they get even better with further treatments?"

"There won't be any more treatments." Kyle looked at Jeopard grimly. "It's all over with." Briefly, trying to sound as unemotional as he could, he explained.

When he finished, Jeopard's blue eyes, so much like his own, were troubled. And yet . . . there was something warmer about them, something more understanding and sympathetic than Kyle had seen in years. Tess reached over and smoothed a strand of damp hair along the nape of Jeopard's neck, her gesture comfortable and loving and intimate. Kyle watched the quick, very private look Jeopard gave her in return. The love in it made him ache for everything he had just lost—or thrown away. He wasn't sure. Lord, he wasn't sure of anything.

Jeopard's gaze came back to him. "The question, little brother, is this: If Sara is telling the truth about her relationship with Valdivia, if it was nothing more than a misguided affair that ended before the kidnapping, then how do you feel about her?"

Kyle shook his head. "She had Valdivia's child nine months after you brought her out of Surador. She was still involved with him right up to the last."

"And she didn't explain why?"

"She wouldn't explain. I've got to find out what she's ashamed or afraid of, what she's still trying to hide."

"And then? Your scars look much better, but you, frankly, look much worse. Pardon me, but you look unhappy as hell."

"Dammit!" Kyle leapt up and began pacing. "I want to trust her! I want to know the rest of what happened between her and Valdivia." He stopped, his shoulders slumped. "There's just so much I don't understand."

"Teodora," Jeopard said suddenly. "See if you can find Teodora Sanchez. She may know something."

"Who was she? The servant in Valdivia's hacienda?"

Jeopard nodded. "The one who helped us with the escape. She was close to both Sara and Dinah. Afterward we helped her get into this country. She's living somewhere in Miami."

Kyle pivoted and started for the door. "I'm on my way to Miami."

"Would it be graceless of me to remind you that Tess and I are getting married in one week, and that you're the best man?"

"I'll be there. I love you." He pulled the front door open and stood there for a moment, looking at the two of them. "I love what you have together. I want the same thing for myself—and Sara."

The beautiful young woman who opened the door had the coloring and features of an Indian, but her eyes were a light, crystalline blue. She wore a white sundress with high-heeled sandals, and the sandals made her tower over Sara even more than she would have towered in bare feet.

"Yes?" she said, smiling first at Sara then at Noelle, who sat in a car seat by Sara's feet. Finally the woman looked at Daisy, who leaned against Sara's legs, on the verge of falling asleep.

Sara cleared her throat. "I'd like to leave a package for Kyle Surprise. I'm Dr. Scarborough."

The blue eyes brightened even more with curiosity. "I'm Tess Gallatin, soon to be Kyle's sister-in-law. In fact, the wedding is tomorrow."

"I won't keep you, then," Sara said quickly. She pointed to a large ice chest that sat on the other side of Noelle's car seat. "That is packed with orchid blossoms. They're very rare orchids, and Kyle uses them—"

"On his face! You should have seen the results!"

Sara swallowed hard. "When?"

"The day he came home from Virginia." The blue eyes filled with compassion. "I don't know all the details of yours and Kyle's problems, but I do think you ought to present the orchids to him your—"

"No, I don't believe that would be best. And . . . my daughter and I are leaving the country tomorrow. We're going to Europe. I don't know when or if we'll be back. So I just wanted to leave these orchids for him."

"Sara." Jeopard Surprise came to the door and stepped outside. He looked at her with some of his old reserve —he would always be the "Iceman" to her—but there was also a gentleness that she'd never seen before. "Kyle's out of town. I don't think he'll be back until tomorrow. Dinah and Rucker are here for the wedding. Stay. See them before you leave the country. Introduce Noelle to them—tell them whatever you think best about her. Dinah was like a sister to you. You owe her a good-bye visit."

Sara stood in the bright sunshine, feeling hot and uncertain and sad. "You're sure that Kyle won't be back until tomorrow?"

"Positive. He's been in Miami all week. I just talked to him a minute ago, and he said he'd be home in the morning."

"All right, then. I'll go get a motel room, and—"

"No." Tess smiled widely. "We'll get you a room on my yacht. All the guests are staying there tonight. We're having a party on board." When Sara looked at her askance, she explained with amusement, "I'm a princess, you see. I have unlimited use of a giant boat."

"All right. As long as someone puts me ashore early in the morning. I don't want to cause any trouble on your wedding day."

Jeopard knelt by Noelle's car seat. Noelle laughed and offered him her pink pacifier. "This trouble looks too sweet to resist."

Sara thought wearily, *I wish that Kyle agreed.*

There was a glittering party on the ship's main deck at sunset, but Sara moved through it woodenly, thinking about the hours she'd spent talking with Dinah and her husband, Rucker, the trust and support they had offered her, and Dinah's distress over her sudden plan to leave the country. Sara had told them everything, knowing that Dinah would believe her because Dinah knew Valdivia so well, and Rucker would believe because he trusted Dinah's intuition.

Sara tried to concentrate on the handsome crowd, the champagne, the caviar, the compliments she received on the beautiful green cocktail dress that Kyle's sister, Millie, had loaned to her. The whispering music of a string ensemble floated on the evening air, and some of the couples were dancing.

It was a happy scene, with Jeopard and Tess at its center. Millie and her husband, Brig McKay, a jovial, mischievous Australian, gave a toast. Erica and Kat, Tess's cousins, offered toasts of their own. Their men, James Tall Wolf and Nathan Chatham, stood beside them, smiling. Audubon had sent an enormous spray of red roses, but the only guest who had any relation to Jeopard and Kyle's former line of work was Drake Lancaster, who had also retired after the Suradoran mission. Drake was with James Tall Wolf's sister, Echo.

Sara felt like the only lonely person in the world, and every second that brought her closer to tomorrow's departure made her heart break a little more from loving Kyle.

When she turned and saw him approaching her through the crowd, she almost collapsed.

His gaze, troubled and determined, met hers and held it as if he intended to hypnotize her. He angled between people, his broad shoulders twisting gracefully inside a dark jacket and pale shirt. His carelessly knotted tie seemed to have suffered from anger, impatience, or both. Tailored, camel-colored trousers sleekly encased his long legs but seemed too civilized for his stride—graceful, stealthy, and filled with the tension of a skilled hunter preparing to capture his prey.

Sara turned swiftly and went to Jeopard. "Kyle has come back early," she told him. "And I'm afraid he's seen me. I'm very sorry that this has happened. There won't be a scene, I promise. I'm going to the nursery and collect my daughter, then wait in my cabin. Can you have a member of the crew take us ashore?"

Kyle spoke behind her. "No."

Sara pivoted and faced him squarely. "Jeopard will explain why I'm here. I didn't plan to see you again. There's no need to be angry. I'm leaving. Good-bye."

"You're not leaving." He took one of her hands in a tight, commanding grip. "I knew you'd be here tonight. Jeopard told me."

Sara looked from one brother to another, her throat constricting with fear. "Why are you trying to trap me? I haven't done anything wrong."

Jeopard squeezed her shoulder gently. "Go with Kyle. You two need to talk in private."

She swiveled her gaze back to Kyle. "I won't answer any more humiliating questions. You've gotten your pound of flesh. Please don't take any more revenge on me and Noelle."

"Let's go talk," Kyle ordered softly, his hand tightening on hers. "We can't discuss this in public."

"I didn't do anything wrong. What do you want, to scrape together so much rumor and innuendo that you can convince a court that what I did for Valdivia constitutes *treason*? Do you despise me that much?"

Kyle leaned toward her, his expression shuttered. "People are beginning to stare. Either come with me voluntarily or I'll scream."

Scream? Flabbergasted, she scrutinized him and found a trace of humor in the set of his mouth. He was enjoying her discomfort, she decided. He was so confident of his ability to make her do what he wanted that he could tease about it.

"Let's get it over with," she said dully. Sara let him lead her away. They went down one level and followed a side deck that fronted the ship's largest cabins. He stopped at a door and unlocked it, still gripping her hand possessively while he did.

Inside he let go of her, locked the door behind them, and flicked a switch that lit a small lamp over a corner bar. Shivering with anxiety, Sara noticed vaguely that the cabin was even more elegant and plush than her own.

"A pretty place for an interrogation," she muttered.

"Sara," he said, his voice weary. He came to her, took both her hands, and looked down at her silently. Sara studied his face and was shocked to find tenderness in it.

She shut her eyes, convinced that she was mistaken. "Your scars are much better."

"Thanks to you."

"Thanks to Mother Nature. I suppose Jeopard told you why I came to Florida. I wanted you to have a supply of orchids. There was no point in letting the blossoms go to waste in the greenhouse."

"You left all your beloved plants uncared for? And your parrots? What about them?"

"I donated everything to a research institute. They're sending people to collect all the plants. And the parrots."

"Where are you planning to go in Europe?"

She shook her head. "I'll travel a lot before I settle down. I'll probably live in England eventually."

"You think you can protect Noelle from the truth about her father by just crossing an ocean?"

"I'm going to try."

His hand squeezed hers, his nimble fingers caressing her palms in a soothing way that made her gaze at him in disbelief. "It won't work," he told her. "The only way to protect Noelle is by teaching her that she's loved for herself, no matter what her father did."

Sara smiled bitterly. "Those are ironic words, coming from you. You can't love her for herself any more than you can love me."

His eyes pinned her with quiet intensity. "You're wrong."

Sara snatched her hands away. "Stop it! A week ago you could barely stand to be in the same room with me. Nothing's changed."

"You're wrong."

"Stop saying that!" Her fists clenched, she backed away. "You set me up from the first day you came to the keep."

He grasped her arms. "I came to you as a friend. It was only at the last that I had to go back to work for Audubon. I did it because I love you. I had to have answers that you wouldn't give."

"You helped Audubon find out about Noelle. You helped him force me to admit things that couldn't help anyone and could only hurt Noelle and me. They hurt you, too, though. You didn't count on that. I tried so hard to protect you. From the very first I tried not to draw you into my life."

He pulled her close to him and stared down into her tear-filled eyes. "The truth hurts like hell, but I'm glad to have it. I'm glad to have *you*."

Stunned, she sank back speechlessly when he let her go. He raised a hand and stroked the backs of his fingers down her cheek. "I know the rest of the truth, now, Tinker Bell. I know what happened between you and Valdivia after the kidnapping."

As his meaning registered, her hands rose to her throat in horror. "What do you think happened?"

"I've been down in Miami all week looking for Teodora Sanchez." He paused and let his hand cup her chin gently. "This morning I finally found her. We had a long conversation about you." His voice dropped to a gruff whisper. "I know what he did to you, sweetheart."

Sara turned away blindly and stumbled to a chair. She sank into it, her head drooping, one hand covering her face. Kyle followed and knelt in front of her. "Did you think I wouldn't believe you?" he asked, his tone low and raspy.

"Yes. Why would you? Why would anyone, after the way I'd been involved with him before the kidnapping?"

"Now I hate the bastard more than I ever could for my own sake."

"He raped me twice," she murmured brokenly. "I threatened to stop working if he touched me again. My research was important to him, so he left me alone." A breath shuddered in her chest. "Until the very last. After I gave him the herbicide, the night before Jeopard and the others came to rescue Dinah and me . . . he decided to . . . *celebrate*, he called it. That was the night that . . . that's why I have Noelle now."

"And you never told anyone except Teodora?"

"I didn't want Dinah to know. She was pregnant, and Valdivia was always tormenting her, always on the verge, we thought, of forcing her into his bed. I couldn't scare her by admitting that he was capable of rape. I didn't want *anyone* to know. I felt as if it were my fault for being such a poor judge of character in the first place." She looked away, angry and humiliated. "Teodora happened to see some bruises on me, and she guessed the truth."

Kyle bowed his head into her lap. His hands gripped the sides of the chair. Sara gazed down at him, tears on her cheeks, her control nearly gone. "From the minute I learned I was pregnant I thought of the baby only as *my* child, never Valdivia's. When I saw you again, at the hospital, I knew I could never explain that to you. I wanted to be with you *so much*, but it was impossible. I didn't want to destroy you; I didn't want you to think that you'd been a fool that day in Valdivia's courtyard. I . . . I didn't want you to hate me."

Tentatively, uncertain about Kyle's feelings for her, she laid a hand on his hair. "Can you understand how I could hate Valdivia and love Noelle? Can you understand how I could love you so much that every lie seemed justified, as long as it protected you from more pain?"

He raised his head. Tears slid between the scars on his face. "Everything you touch is filled with magic. I understand."

"Everything?" she asked, her tone soft and desperate. She laid one hand along his face. "Is there enough magic to keep you from thinking about Valdivia when you look at me? When you touch me?"

"I'll show you." He stood, lifted her to her feet, then picked her up. He carried her to the bed and lay down beside her. Gently he cupped her face, held it, and kissed her with slow, sweet devotion.

Sara broke from his embrace and, crying, twisted away from him. "I never expected you to accept it. Don't be kind to me out of sympathy or guilt. I need you to love me the way you did before you found out the truth."

"That's what I'm trying to do," he said as his quick, agile hands unzipped the back of her dress. "I'm going to show you that nothing's changed, sweetheart."

He peeled her dress down to her elbows and began kissing her shoulders. Slowly he slid his hand around her and stroked her breasts through slip and bra. She shivered and remained huddled with her back to him. He made a low sound of distress. "You have to show me that you haven't changed either. I know you must resent me for the way I've interfered in your life. I don't blame you for having a lot of second thoughts about me."

"Not second thoughts. Just the fear that"—her voice nearly deserted her, and she could barely whisper—"just the fear that Valdivia has taken something away from us that we'll never get back."

Kyle turned her to face him and looked down at her with anguished eyes. "Are you going to let him win? Or are you going to trust me? Are you going to believe that I love you *more* now than before?"

"Oh, Kyle."

"I want to make you happy, and I know I can do it. He never made you happy and never could. He didn't deserve you, and despite all the grief I've caused you in the past few weeks, I'm selfish enough to think that I do deserve you. *That's* my victory."

She cried and put her arms around his neck. "Be selfish. Let's fight him together. Let's chase the memories away forever." She pulled Kyle to her for an adoring, tear-dampened kiss.

He loved her like sunshine loves the dawn, chasing the darkness away moment by moment with his whispers and his touch, filling her until she glowed with shared power. Afterward they lay spellbound and silent, clothes jumbled around them as if they'd tried to build a nest, their faces nuzzled close together. He brought her hand up and drew it over his scars, still so vivid. "They're gone," he promised.

Sara brushed her lips across his face. "I never saw them to begin with."

A little later they dressed and solemnly assured each other that no one would suspect, from looking at them, that they'd been making love. He put his arm around her and they left the cabin. Sara rested her head on his shoulder and latched both arms around his waist.

Strolling along a side deck through the darkness of a warm night, they gazed at the ocean and the sky. A full moon hung there like a silver ornament. "I'm sure the keep must be full of elves tonight," Kyle told her. "And they're wondering where their queen and princess have run off to. Do you think the elves could get used to having an ordinary human around all the time?"

"I don't know what ordinary human you mean." She tilted her head back and looked at him in the enchanted moonlight. "I know they'd love a dragonslayer like you, though."

"Speaking of dragons, you'll be happy to know that your geese trapped Audubon in a tree."

"Oh, no!" But she couldn't help smiling thinly. "I'm so pleased."

Both of them laughed then, and kissed each other gently. "Wait here," she told Kyle. "I'm going to the nursery and get Noelle. You keep our place in the moonlight."

Very soon she returned, Noelle in her arms. Sara watched Kyle's face anxiously as she came to a stop beside him. Daisy padded up and flopped by their feet; she would always guard her people, and she would always remind them that dragons can be good, and loving.

Noelle squealed with delight and held out her arms to Kyle. "How do you feel about her?" Sara asked, her throat tight.

Tears of happiness rose in Sara's eyes as he took her daughter and cradled her in a tender, protective embrace. He slid the other arm around Sara. Noelle bowed her head to theirs in the moonlight. "Cal," she whispered in wonder, as if caught in the magic of the moon.

"There's one thing we have to do right away," Kyle said.

Sara lovingly laid one hand against Noelle's cheek and the other against his. "Yes?"

He hugged them closer to his heart. "Teach her to say *daddy*."

THE EDITOR'S CORNER

1990. A new decade. I suspect that most of us who are involved in romance publishing will remember the 1980s as "the romance decade." During the past ten years we have seen a momentous change as Americans jumped into the romance business and developed the talent and expertise to publish short, contemporary American love stories. Previously the only romances of this type had come from British and Australian authors through the Canadian company, Harlequin Enterprises. That lonely giant, or monopoly, was first challenged in the early 1980s when Dell published Ecstasy romances under Vivien Stephens's direction; by Simon and Schuster, which established Silhouette romances (now owned by Harlequin); and by Berkley/Jove, which supported my brainchild, Second Chance at Love. After getting that line off to a fine start, I came to Bantam.

The times had grown turbulent by the middle of the decade. But an industry had been born. Editors who liked and understood romance had been found and trained. Enormous numbers of writers had been discovered and were flocking to workshops and seminars sponsored by the brand-new Romance Writers of America to acquire or polish their skills.

LOVESWEPT was launched with six romances in May 1983. And I am extremely proud of all the wonderful authors who've been with us through these seven years and who have never left the fold, no matter the inducements to do so. I'm just as proud of the LOVESWEPT staff. There's been very little turnover—Susann Brailey, Nita Taublib, and Elizabeth Barrett have been on board all along; Carrie Feron and Tom Kleh have been here a year and two years, respectively. I'm also delighted by you, our readers, who have so wholeheartedly endorsed every innovation we've dared to make—our authors publishing under their real names and including pictures and autobiographies in their books, and the Fan of the Month feature, which puts the spotlight on a person who represents many of our readers. And of course I thank you for all your kind words about the Editor's Corner.

Now, starting this new decade, we find there wasn't enough growth in the audience for romances and/or there was too much being published, so that most American publishers have left the arena. It is only big Harlequin and little LOVESWEPT. Despite our small size, we are as vigorous and hearty, excited and exuberant now as we were in the beginning. I can't wait to see what the next ten years bring. What LOVESWEPT innova-

(continued)

tions do you imagine I might be summarizing in the Editor's Corner as we head into the new *century*?

But now to turn from musings about the year 2000 to the very real pleasures of next month!

Let Iris Johansen take you on one of her most thrilling, exciting journeys to Sedikhan, read **NOTORIOUS,** LOVESWEPT #378. It didn't matter to Sabin Wyatt that the jury had acquitted gorgeous actress Mallory Thane of his stepbrother's murder. She had become his obsession. He cleverly gets her to Sedikhan and confronts her with a demand that she tell him the truth about her marriage. When she does, he refuses to believe her story. He will believe only what he can feel: primitive, consuming desire for Mallory. . . . Convinced that Mallory returns his passion, Sabin takes her in fiery and unforgettable moments. That's only the beginning of **NOTORIOUS,** which undoubtedly is going onto my list of all-time favorites from Iris. I bet you, too, will label this romance a keeper.

Here comes another of Gail Douglas's fabulous romances about the sisters, *The Dreamweavers,* whose stories never fail to enmesh me and hold me spellbound. In LOVESWEPT #379, **SOPHISTICATED LADY,** we meet the incredible jazz pianist Pete Cochrane. When he looks up from the keyboard into Lisa Sinclair's eyes, he is captivated by the exquisite honey-blonde. He begins to play Ellington's "Sophisticated Lady," and Ann is stunned by the potent appeal of this musical James Bond. These two vagabonds have a rocky road to love that we think you'll relish every step of the way.

What a delight to welcome back Jan Hudson with her LOVESWEPT #380, **ALWAYS FRIDAY.** Full of fun and laced with fire, **ALWAYS FRIDAY** introduces us to handsome executive Daniel Friday and darling Tess Cameron. From the very first, Tess knows that there's no one better to unstarch Dan's collars and teach him to cut loose from his workaholism. Dan fears he can't protect his free-spirited and sexy Tess from disappointment. It's a glorious set of problems these two confront and solve.

Next, in Peggy Webb's **VALLEY OF FIRE,** LOVESWEPT #381, you are going to meet a dangerous man. A very dangerous and exciting man. I'd be surprised if you didn't find Rick McGill, the best private investigator in Tupelo, Mississippi, the stuff that the larger-than-life Sam Spades are made of with a little Valentino thrown in. Martha Ann Riley summons all her courage to dare to play Bacall to Rick's Bogart. She wants to find her sister's gambler husband . . . and turns out to be Rick's

(continued)

perfect companion for a sizzling night in a cave, a wicked romp through Las Vegas. Wildly attracted, Martha Ann thinks Rick is the most irresistible scoundrel she's ever met . . . and the most untrustworthy! Don't miss **VALLEY OF FIRE!** It's fantastic.

Glenna McReynolds gives us her most ambitious and thrilling romance to date in LOVESWEPT #382, **DATELINE: KYDD AND RIOS.** Nobody knew more about getting into trouble than Nikki Kydd, but that talent had made her perfect at finding stories for Josh Rios, the daring photojournalist who'd built his career reporting the battles and betrayals of San Simeon's dictatorship. After three years as partners, when he could resist her no longer, he ordered Nikki back to the States—but in the warm, dark tropical night he couldn't let her go . . . without teaching the green-eyed witch her power as a woman. She'd vanished with the dawn rather than obey Josh's command to leave, but now, a year later, Nikki needs him back . . . to fulfill a desperate bargain.

What a treat you can expect from Fayrene Preston next month—the launch book of her marvelous quartet about the people who live and work in a fabulous house, SwanSea Place. Here in LOVESWEPT #383, *SwanSea Place:* **THE LEGACY,** Caitlin Deverell had been born in SwanSea, the magnificent family home on the wild, windswept coast of Maine, and now she was restoring its splendor to open it as a luxury resort. When Nico DiFrenza asked her to let him stay for a few days, caution demanded she refuse the mysterious visitor's request—but his spellbinding charm made that impossible! So begins a riveting tale full of the unique charm Fayrene can so wonderfully invent for us.

Altogether a spectacular start to the new decade with great LOVESWEPT reading.

Warm good wishes,

Carolyn Nichols

Carolyn Nichols
Editor
LOVESWEPT
Bantam Books
666 Fifth Avenue
New York, NY 10103

FAN OF THE MONTH

Hazel Parker

Twelve years ago my husband Hoke insisted that I quit my job as a data processor to open a paperback bookstore. The reason was that our book bill had become as large as our grocery bill. Today I am still in the book business, in a much larger store, still reading and selling my favorite romance novels.

My most popular authors are of course writing for what I consider to be the number one romance series— LOVESWEPT. One of the all-time favorites is Kay Hooper. Her books appeal to readers because of her sense of humor and unique characters (for instance, Pepper in **PEPPER'S WAY**). And few authors can write better books than Iris Johansen's **THE TRUST-WORTHY REDHEAD** or Fayrene Preston's **FOR THE LOVE OF SAMI.** When the three authors get together (as they did for the Delaney series), you have *dynamite*. Keep up the good work, LOVESWEPT.

60 Minutes to a Better, More Beautiful You!

Now it's easier than ever to awaken your sensuality, stay slim forever—even make yourself irresistible. With Bantam's bestselling subliminal audio tapes, you're only 60 minutes away from a better, more beautiful you!

NEW!

Handsome Book Covers Specially Designed To Fit Loveswept Books

Our new French Calf Vinyl book covers come in a set of three great colors—royal blue, scarlet red and kachina green.

Each 7" × 9½" book cover has two deep vertical pockets, a handy sewn-in bookmark, and is soil and scratch resistant.

To order your set, use the form below.

THE DELANEY DYNASTY

Men and women whose loves an passions are so glorious it takes many great romance novels by three bestselling authors to tell their tempestuous stories.

THE SHAMROCK TRINITY

☐	21975	**RAFE, THE MAVERICK** *by Kay Hooper*	$2.95
☐	21976	**YORK, THE RENEGADE** *by Iris Johansen*	$2.95
☐	21977	**BURKE, THE KINGPIN** *by Fayrene Preston*	$2.95

THE DELANEYS OF KILLAROO

☐	21872	**ADELAIDE, THE ENCHANTRESS** *by Kay Hooper*	$2.75
☐	21873	**MATILDA, THE ADVENTURESS** *by Iris Johansen*	$2.75
☐	21874	**SYDNEY, THE TEMPTRESS** *by Fayrene Preston*	$2.75

THE DELANEYS: *The Untamed Years*

☐	21899	**GOLDEN FLAMES** *by Kay Hooper*	$3.50
☐	21898	**WILD SILVER** *by Iris Johansen*	$3.50
☐	21897	**COPPER FIRE** *by Fayrene Preston*	$3.50

Buy them at your local bookstore or use this page to order.

Bantam Books, Dept. SW7, 414 East Golf Road, Des Plaines, IL 60016

Please send me the items I have checked above. I am enclosing $_____ (please add $2.00 to cover postage and handling). Send check or money order, no cash or C.O.D.s please.

Mr/Ms _____

Address _____

City/State _____ Zip_____

SW7–11/89

Please allow four to six weeks for delivery.
Prices and availability subject to change without notice.

THE LATEST IN BOOKS AND AUDIO CASSETTES

Paperbacks

☐	27032	**FIRST BORN** Doris Mortman	$4.95
☐	27283	**BRAZEN VIRTUE** Nora Roberts	$3.95
☐	25891	**THE TWO MRS. GRENVILLES** Dominick Dunne	$4.95
☐	27891	**PEOPLE LIKE US** Dominick Dunne	$4.95
☐	27260	**WILD SWAN** Celeste De Blasis	$4.95
☐	25692	**SWAN'S CHANCE** Celeste De Blasis	$4.50
☐	26543	**ACT OF WILL** Barbara Taylor Bradford	$5.95
☐	27790	**A WOMAN OF SUBSTANCE** Barbara Taylor Bradford	$5.95

Audio

☐ **THE SHELL SEEKERS** by Rosamunde Pilcher
Performance by Lynn Redgrave
180 Mins. Double Cassette   48183-9 $14.95

☐ **THE NAKED HEART** by Jacqueline Briskin
Performance by Stockard Channing
180 Mins. Double Cassette   45169-3 $14.95

☐ **COLD SASSY TREE** by Olive Ann Burns
Performance by Richard Thomas
180 Mins. Double Cassette   45166-9 $14.95

☐ **PEOPLE LIKE US** by Dominick Dunne
Performance by Len Cariou
180 Mins. Double Cassette   45164-2 $14.95

Bantam Books, Dept. FBS, 414 East Golf Road, Des Plaines, IL 60016

Please send me the items I have checked above. I am enclosing $_____
(please add $2.00 to cover postage and handling). Send check or money
order, no cash or C.O.D.s please.

Mr/Ms _____

Address _____

City/State _____ Zip_____

Please allow four to six weeks for delivery.
Prices and availability subject to change without notice.

FBS–11/89